THE ABOMINABLE SNOWMAN OF PASADENA

Look for more Goosebumps books
by R.L. Stine:
(see back of book for a complete listing)

Goosebumps®

THE ABOMINABLE SNOWMAN OF PASADENA

R.L. STINE

AN
APPLE
PAPERBACK

SCHOLASTIC INC.
New York Toronto London Auckland Sydney

A PARACHUTE PRESS BOOK

ISBN 0-590-56875-2

12 11 10 9 8 7 6 5 4 3 2   5 6 7 8 9/9 0/0

Printed in the U.S.A.   40

First Scholastic printing, December 1995

1

All my life, I've wanted to see snow.

My name is Jordan Blake. My life has been twelve years of sun, sand, and chlorine. I'd never felt cold, *ever* — unless you count air-conditioned supermarkets. And I don't. It doesn't snow in the supermarket.

I'd never felt cold, that is, until the adventure.

Some people think I'm a lucky guy to live in Pasadena, California, where it's always sunny and warm. It's okay, I guess. But if you've never seen snow, it seems like something out of a science-fiction movie.

Fluffy white frozen water that falls out of the sky? It piles up on the ground, and you can make forts and snowmen and snowballs out of it? You have to admit it sounds weird.

One day, my wish came true. I got to see snow at last. And it turned out to be weirder than I thought.

Way weirder.

"Pay attention, kids. This is going to be cool."

Dad's face glowed under the red darkroom light. My sister, Nicole, and I watched him developing film. With a pair of tongs, he dipped a sheet of special paper in a chemical bath.

I've watched Dad develop film all my life. He's a professional photographer. But I'd never seen him so excited about photos before — and that's saying a lot.

Dad takes nature photos. Well, actually, he takes pictures of *everything*!

He never *stops* taking pictures. My mom says that once when I was a baby I saw Dad and screamed. I didn't recognize him without a camera in front of his face. I used to think he had a zoom lens for a nose!

Our house is filled with embarrassing pictures of me — me as a baby in baggy diapers, me with food all over my face, me crying after scraping my knee, me hitting my sister . . .

Anyway, Dad had just returned from a trip to the Grand Tetons. That's a mountain range in Wyoming — part of the Rocky Mountains. He was all worked up about the pictures he took there.

"I wish you kids had seen those bears," Dad said. "A whole family of them. The cubs reminded me of you two — always teasing each other."

Teasing. Ha. Dad thinks Nicole and I *tease* each other. That's putting it mildly. Nicole — Miss Know-it-all — drives me crazy.

2

Sometimes I wish she'd never been born. I've made it my mission to make *her* feel the same way. I mean, I try to make her wish she'd never been born.

"You should have taken us with you to the Grand Tetons, Dad," I complained.

"It's very cold in Wyoming this time of year," Nicole said.

"How do you know, Brainiac?" I jabbed her in the ribs. "You've never been to Wyoming."

"I read up on it while Dad was away," she explained. Of course. "There's a picture book about it in the library if you want to know more, Jordan. It's just right for you — it's for first graders."

I couldn't think of anything to say back. That's my problem. I'm too slow with the comebacks. So I jabbed her again.

"Hey, hey," Dad murmured. "No jabbing. I'm working here."

Dumb Nicole. Not that she's dumb — she's really smart. But in a dumb way — that's my opinion. She's so smart she skipped fifth grade — and landed in *my* class. She's a year younger than I am and she's in my class — *and* she gets straight A's.

Dad's pictures floated in the chemical bath, slowly becoming clear. "Did it snow in the mountains while you were there, Dad?" I asked.

"Sure, it snowed," Dad replied. He was concentrating on his work.

"Did you go skiing?" I asked.

Dad shook his head. "I was too busy working."

"How about ice-skating?" Nicole asked.

Nicole acts as if she knows everything. But like me, she'd never seen snow, either. We'd never left Southern California — and you could tell by looking at us.

We're both tan all year round. Nicole's hair is greenish-blond from the chlorine in the community pool, and mine is brown with blond streaks. We're on the school swim team.

"I'll bet it's snowing at Mom's house right now," Nicole said.

"Could be," Dad replied.

Mom and Dad are divorced. Mom just moved to Pennsylvania. We're going to spend the summer with her. But we stayed in California with Dad to finish out the school year.

Mom sent us some pictures of her new house. It was covered with snow. I stared at the pictures, trying to imagine the cold.

"I wish we stayed at Mom's house while you were gone," I said.

"Jordan, we've been over this." Dad sounded a little impatient. "You can visit your mother when she's settled. She hasn't even bought furniture yet. Where would you sleep?"

"I'd rather sleep on a bare floor than listen to Mrs. Witchens snoring on the couch," I grumbled.

Mrs. Witchens stayed with Nicole and me while Dad was away. She was a nightmare. Every morning we had to clean our rooms — she actually inspected them for dust. Every single night she served us liver, brussels sprouts, and fish-head soup with a tall glass of soy milk.

"Her name's not *Witchens*," Nicole corrected me. "It's *Hitchens*."

"I *know* that, *Si*cole," I retorted.

Under the red light in the darkroom, the photos grew clearer. I heard excitement in Dad's voice.

"If these shots come out well, I can publish them in a book," he said. "I will call it *The Brown Bears of Wyoming*, by Garrison Blake. Yes, that has a nice ring to it."

He stopped to pull a photo out of the liquid. It dripped as he stared at it.

"That's weird," he murmured.

"What's weird?" Nicole asked.

He set the picture down without saying anything. Nicole and I glanced at it.

"Dad — " Nicole said. "I hate to break it to you, but that looks like a teddy bear."

It *was* a picture of a teddy bear. A stuffed brown toy bear with a lopsided grin, sitting in the grass. Not the kind of creature you usually find in the Grand Tetons.

"There must be some mistake," Dad said. "Wait until the rest of the photos develop. You'll see. They're amazing."

He pulled up another picture. He studied it. "Huh?"

I grabbed the photo. Another teddy bear.

Dad picked up a third picture. Then a fourth. He moved faster and faster.

"More teddy bears!" he cried. He was frantic. Even in the darkroom, I could see the panic on his face.

"What's going on?" he shouted. "Where are the photos I took?"

2

"Dad — " Nicole began. "Are you *sure* those bears you saw were real?"

"Of course I'm sure!" Dad boomed at her. "I know the difference between a brown bear and a teddy bear!"

He began to pace back and forth across the darkroom floor. "Did I lose the film somehow?" he murmured, clutching his head with one hand. "Could someone have switched it?"

"The weird part is that you were taking pictures of bears," Nicole noted. "And you ended up with *teddy* bears. That's just so strange."

Dad furiously tapped his hands on the developing table. He muttered to himself. He was starting to lose it.

"Did I lose the film on the plane somehow? Switch carry-on bags with someone else, maybe?"

I turned my back to Dad, my shoulders shaking.

"Jordan? What's the matter?" Dad grabbed my shoulders. "Are you all right?"

7

He spun me around. "Jordan!" Dad cried. "You're — laughing!"

Nicole crossed her arms. She narrowed her eyes at me. "What did you do to Dad's pictures?"

Dad frowned. His voice was calmer now. "All right, Jordan. What's the big joke?"

I gasped for breath, trying to stop laughing. "Don't worry, Dad. Your pictures are okay."

He shoved one of the teddy bear shots in my face. "Okay! You call this okay?!"

"I borrowed your camera before you left for Wyoming," I explained. "I took a bunch of shots of my old teddy bear, for a joke. The rest of the film should have your real bears on it."

I can't resist a good practical joke.

Nicole said, "I had nothing to do with it, Dad. I swear."

Little Miss Goody-Goody.

Dad shook his head. "A joke?" He turned back to the photos and developed a few more. The next shot showed a real bear cub fishing in a stream. Dad laughed.

"You know," he said, putting the picture of the real bear next to one of the teddy bear shots, "they don't look as different as you'd think."

I knew Dad wouldn't stay angry. He never does. That's one reason I like to play tricks on him. He likes to play practical jokes, too.

"Did I ever tell you about the trick I pulled on

Joe Morrison?" he asked. Joe Morrison is a photographer friend of Dad's.

"Joe had just gotten back from Africa, where he had spent months photographing gorillas. He was all excited about these fabulous gorilla shots he'd taken. I saw the pictures, and they were really spectacular.

"Joe had a big meeting set up with the editor of a nature magazine. He was going to go in and show the editor these photos. He was sure the magazine would snap them up in a second.

"Joe didn't know that the editor and I had gone to college together. So I called her up and asked her to help me play a little joke on Joe.

"When Joe went to see her, he showed her the pictures. She looked at them without saying a word.

"Finally he couldn't stand the suspense any longer. He blurted out, 'Well? Do you like them or not?' He's an impatient guy, Joe."

"What did she say?" I asked.

"She frowned and said, 'You're a good photographer, Mr. Morrison. But I'm afraid you've been tricked. The creatures you photographed aren't gorillas at all.'

"Joe's jaw practically fell off his face. He said, 'What do you mean, they're not gorillas?'

"She said, with a perfectly straight face, 'They're people in gorilla suits. Can't you tell the difference between a real gorilla and a man in a gorilla suit, Mr. Morrison?' "

I chuckled. Nicole asked, "Then what happened?"

"Joe practically had a nervous breakdown. He snatched up the photos and stared at them. He shouted, 'I don't get it! How could that happen? I spent six months of my life studying people in gorilla suits?'

"Finally the editor burst out laughing and told him it was a joke. She loved the photos and wanted to publish them. Joe wouldn't believe her at first — it took her fifteen minutes to get him to calm down."

Dad and I both laughed.

"I think that's really mean, Dad," Nicole scolded.

I get my joker streak from Dad. Nicole takes after Mom. She's more practical.

"Joe thought it was funny once he got over the shock," Dad assured her. "He's played his share of tricks on me, believe me."

Dad swished another photo through the chemical bath. Then he held it up with his tongs. It showed two bear cubs wrestling. He smiled with satisfaction.

"This roll came out great," he said. "But I've got a lot more work to do in here, kids. Go on outside for a while, okay?"

He turned the red light off and flipped on the normal light. Nicole opened the door.

"Don't get all messed up and dirty, though," Dad added. "We're all going out to dinner tonight. I want to celebrate my luck with the brown bears."

"We'll be careful," Nicole promised.

"Speak for yourself," I said.

"I mean it, Jordan," Dad warned.

"Just kidding, Dad."

A wave of heat blasted us when we opened the darkroom door. Nicole and I stepped out into the backyard, blinking in the afternoon sun. It always takes my eyes a long time to adjust after I've been in the darkroom.

"What do you want to do?" Nicole asked.

"I don't know," I replied. "It's so hot. It's too hot to do much of anything."

Nicole closed her eyes and zoned out for a minute.

"Nicole?" I nudged her. "Nicole? What are you doing?"

"I'm thinking about the snow in Dad's pictures of the Grand Tetons. I thought it would make me feel cooler."

She stood perfectly still with her eyes closed. A bead of sweat dripped down her forehead.

"Well?" I asked. "Is it working?"

She opened her eyes and shook her head. "No. How can I imagine snow if I've never felt it?"

"Good point." I sighed and gazed around me.

We live in a subdivision in the suburbs of Pasadena. There are only three different kinds of houses in our neighborhood. The same three house styles are repeated for miles around.

It's so boring to look at, it makes me feel even hotter, somehow. Each block has a couple of palm trees, not enough to give much shade. There's a vacant lot across the street from us, next door to the Millers'. The most exciting feature of our backyard — maybe the whole block — is Dad's disgusting compost heap.

I squinted and stared some more. Everything appeared bleached in the sunlight. Even the grass looked almost white.

"I'm so bored I could scream," I complained.

"Let's ride our bikes," Nicole suggested. "Maybe the breeze will cool us off."

"Maybe Lauren will want to go with us," I added.

Lauren Sax lives next door to us. She's in our class at school. I see her so often, she might as well be my sister.

We rolled out our bikes from the garage and walked them over to Lauren's. We left our bikes at the side of her house. Then we went around back.

We found Lauren sitting on a towel under a palm tree in her backyard. Nicole sat beside Lauren on the towel. I leaned against the tree.

12

"It's so hot!" Lauren whined. She tugged on her yellow shorts. She's tall and muscular, with long brown hair and bangs.

She has a nasal voice, good for complaining. "This is supposed to be winter. It's winter everywhere else. A normal winter has snow and ice and sleet and freezing rain and cold, cold air. What do we get? Nothing but sun! Why do we have to be so *hot*?"

Suddenly I felt a pain in my back.

"Ow!" I jerked forward. Something stabbed me. Something stinging sharp — and ice cold! My face twisted in pain.

"Jordan!" Nicole gasped. "What's wrong? What's wrong?"

3

I clutched the icy spot on my back. "What is it?" I cried. "It's so cold!"

Nicole jumped to her feet and examined my back. "Jordan, you've been stabbed!" she announced. "With a purple Popsicle!"

As I turned around I heard mean laughter. The Miller twins jumped out from behind the tree.

I should've known. The Miller twins — Kyle and Kara. The twin pug noses, the beady little eyes, the matching short-cropped red hair. Yuck. They carried twin Super Soakers, red ones.

The Miller twins love practical jokes. They're worse than I am. And much meaner.

Everyone in the neighborhood is afraid of them. They pounce on little kids waiting at the bus stop and rob them of their lunch money. Once they blew up the Saxes' mailbox with a stink bomb. Last year, Kyle sucker-punched me during a basketball game. He thought it was funny to watch me turn purple.

The Millers like to pick on me more than anyone, for some reason.

Kara is just as scary as her brother Kyle. I hate to admit it, but Kara can take me out with one punch. I know that for a fact. She gave me a black eye last summer.

" 'Oh, it's so hot. It's so hot!' " Kara sneered, making fun of Lauren's whiny voice.

Kyle flipped his Super Soaker from one hand to the other behind his back. He tried to make it look like a really complicated move.

"Arnold taught me how to do that," he bragged.

Kyle wanted me to think he was talking about Arnold Schwarzenegger. He claims he knows Arnold. I have my doubts.

Nicole tugged on the back of my shirt. "Dad's going to kill you, Jordan," she said.

"Why?"

I craned my neck backwards. The back of my white polo shirt was stained dark purple.

"Oh, great," I muttered.

"Dad said not to get messed up," Nicole reminded me. As if I needed to be reminded.

"Don't worry, Jordan," Kyle said. "We'll clean it off for you."

"Uh — that's okay," I murmured, backing away. Whatever Kyle meant by "clean it off," I knew I wouldn't like it.

15

I was right.

He and Kara raised their Super Soakers and squirted me, Nicole, and Lauren.

"Stop it!" Lauren screamed. "You're getting us all wet!"

Kyle and Kara laughed their maniac laughs. "You *said* you were hot!"

They drenched us. My shirt was so wet I could wring a glass of water out of it. I glared at them.

Kyle shrugged. "We were only trying to help."

Yeah. Sure they were.

I should've been grateful that all they did was soak us. We got off easy.

I can't stand the Miller twins. Neither can Nicole and Lauren. They think they're so hot. Just because they're thirteen and they have a swimming pool in their backyard.

Their father works at a movie studio. They're always bragging about how they go to sneak previews and hang out with movie stars.

I haven't seen a movie star show up at their house yet. Not once.

"Aw, you're all wet," Kara said, sneering. "Why don't you take a bike ride to dry off?"

Nicole and I exchanged glances. When we're alone, we don't get along so well. But when the Millers are around, we have to stick together.

We knew the Millers too well. They wouldn't mention our bikes without a reason. A bad reason.

"What did you do to our bikes?" Nicole demanded.

The Millers faked wide-eyed innocence. "Who — us? We didn't do anything to your precious bikes. Go see for yourself."

Nicole and I glanced around the side of Lauren's house, where we'd left our bikes.

"They look okay from here," Nicole whispered.

"There's something wrong with them," I said. "They look weird."

We approached our bikes. They looked weird all right. The handlebars had been unscrewed and twisted backwards.

"Hope you have reverse gear," Kyle snickered.

Normally, I'm not the kind of guy who goes around getting into fights. But something in me snapped. This time Kyle and Kara had gone too far.

I jumped on Kyle. We tumbled to the ground. We wrestled. I tried to pin him with my knee, but he pushed me over onto my side.

"Stop it!" Nicole screamed. "Stop it!"

Kyle rolled me onto my back. "You thought you could jump me, Jordan? You're too big a wimp!"

I kicked him. He pinned my shoulder to the ground with one knee.

Nicole shouted hysterically, "Jordan! Look out!"

I glanced up. Kara stood over me, clutching a rock the size of her head. A mean grin spread across her face.

"Drop it, Kara!" Kyle ordered.

I tried to roll out of the way, but I couldn't move. Kyle had me pinned.

Kara heaved the rock. Then she let it drop — right onto my head.

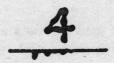

4

I squeezed my eyes shut.

The rock landed on my forehead — and bounced off.

I opened my eyes. Kara laughed like a hyena. She picked up the rock and dropped it on my face again. It bounced off, just like the first time.

Lauren grabbed it. "It's made of sponge," she announced. She squeezed it in her hand. "It's a fake."

Kyle laughed. "It's a movie prop, moron."

"You should've seen your face," Kara added. "What a chicken!"

I kicked Kyle off me and pounced on him again. This time I was so mad I had the strength of two Kyles. I wrestled him to the ground. I had him pinned!

"What's going on, guys?"

Uh-oh. Dad.

I leaped to my feet. "Hi, Dad. We were just kidding around."

Kyle sat up, rubbing his elbow.

Dad didn't even seem to notice that we'd been fighting. He was excited about something.

"Listen, kids — I have great news. *Wilderness* magazine just called. They want to fly me to Alaska!"

"Great, Dad," I said sarcastically. "You get to go on another exciting trip while we stay here and die of boredom."

"And heat," Nicole added.

Dad laughed. "I called Mrs. Hitchens to see if she could come stay with you again — " he began.

"Not Mrs. Hitchens again!" I cried. "Dad, she's horrible! I can't stand her cooking. I'll starve to death if she stays with us!"

"You will not, Jordan," Nicole said. "Even if you ate only bread and water, you could survive a week easily."

"Nicole? Jordan? Hello?" Dad said, knocking lightly on our heads. "Will you please listen to me? I haven't finished yet."

"Sorry, Dad."

"Anyway, Mrs. Hitchens can't come. So, I guess you two will just have to come along with me."

"To Alaska?" I cried. I was too excited to believe it.

"Hurray!" Nicole yelled. We jumped up and down.

"You guys are so lucky!" Lauren said. Kara and Kyle stood by. Saying nothing.

"We're going to Alaska!" I shouted. "We'll get to see snow! Tons of snow! Alaskan snow!"

I was thrilled. And Dad hadn't even told us the interesting part yet.

"It's a strange project," Dad continued. "They want me to track down some kind of snow creature — an Abominable Snowman."

"Wow!" I gasped.

Kyle and Kara snorted.

Nicole shook her head. "An Abominable Snowman? Has anybody really seen him?"

Dad nodded. "Some kind of snow creature has been spotted. Who knows what it really is. Whatever it is, the magazine wants me to shoot photos of it. I'm sure it's a wild-goose chase. There's no such thing as an Abominable Snowman."

"So why are you going?" Nicole asked.

I poked her in the ribs. "Who cares? We're going to Alaska!"

"The magazine is paying a big fee," Dad explained. "And even if we don't find a snow creature, I'll still get some great shots of the tundra."

Lauren asked, "What's a tundra?"

Dad began to reply, but Nicole stepped forward. "I'll handle this one, Dad," she interrupted. I felt like screaming. She does that in school all the time, too.

"A tundra is a huge frozen plain. It exists in the Arctic, in Alaska, and in Russia. The word *tundra* comes from the Russian, meaning — "

I clapped my hand over her big mouth. "Any other questions, Lauren?"

Lauren shook her head. "That's all I needed to know."

"Egghead here goes on forever if you don't stop her." I let go of Nicole's mouth. She stuck her tongue out at me.

"This trip is going to be great," I cried happily. "We'll see ice and snow for real! We're going hunting for an Abominable Snowman! Awesome!"

An hour earlier we'd been bored out of our minds. Now suddenly everything had changed.

Dad smiled. "I've got to go back to the darkroom for a while. Don't forget — we're going out to dinner tonight." He wandered back across the lawn and into the house.

As soon as Dad was gone, Kara started laughing. "An Abominable Snowman! What a joke!"

Typical Kara — she was too chicken to say a word while Dad was around.

Kyle made fun of me, jumping up and down and squealing, "Alaska! Alaska! I'll get to see snow!"

"You both will probably turn blue and freeze," Kara sneered.

"*We'll* be fine," Nicole said. "It's *your* turn to freeze!" She grabbed Kara's Super Soaker and sent a spray of water into Kara's face.

22

"Stop it!" Kyle shouted. He dove at Nicole. Nicole laughed and ran away, turning around to soak them every few feet.

"Give that back!" Kara yelled.

The Millers chased Nicole. Kyle raised his Super Soaker and let Nicole have it in the back.

Lauren and I ran after them. Nicole raced into our backyard. She turned around and squirted the Millers again.

"You can't catch me!" she cried, shooting and walking backward.

She was backing right into Dad's compost heap.

Should I warn her? I thought.

No way.

"Take that!" she shouted, blasting the Millers with water.

Then she slipped and fell backward — into the compost heap.

"Yuck," Lauren groaned.

Nicole stood up slowly. Greenish-brown slime oozed in her hair and dripped down her back, her arms, and her legs. "Ugh!" she screamed, frantically wiping the glop off her hands. "Uggghhh!"

We all stood and stared. She looked like some kind of Abominable Snowman herself. All covered in glop.

We were still staring when Dad popped his head out the back door. "You kids ready to go to dinner?" he called.

5

"There it is!" Dad shouted over the roar of the small plane's engine. "Iknek. That's the airstrip."

I stared out the window at the tiny brown patch where we'd be landing. For the last half hour I'd seen nothing but miles and miles of snow. Wow. It was so *white*!

It was cool the way the snow sparkled in the sunlight. It made me think of Christmas carols. I couldn't get "Winter Wonderland" out of my head — and it was driving me crazy!

I watched for giant footprints as we flew. How big would an Abominable Snowman's footsteps be? Big enough to see from a low-flying plane?

"I hope there's a restaurant down there," Nicole said. "I'm starving."

Dad patted her shoulder. "We'll have a big, hot meal before we set out. But after that, it's camping food."

"How are we going to build a fire in the snow?" Nicole asked.

"We'll be staying in a little cabin," Dad replied. "It's a long way out in the tundra, but it's better than sleeping in tents. There should be a stove in the cabin. I *hope* so, anyway."

"Can we build an igloo and sleep in that?" I asked. "Or dig out an ice cave?"

"You can't build an igloo just like that, Jordan," Nicole snapped. "It's not like a snow fort or something. Right, Dad?"

Dad took the lens cap off his camera and started taking pictures through the plane window. "Sure," he said absently. "Uh-huh."

Nicole turned to the window, too. I mimicked her behind her back. *You can't build an igloo just like that,* I mouthed. She acts like she's my teacher or something. It's really embarrassing when she does it in front of everybody at school.

"How are we going to find the cabin?" Nicole asked. "Everything looks the same in all this snow."

Dad turned and snapped a picture of her. "Did you say something, Nicole?"

"I was wondering how we're going to find the cabin," Nicole repeated. "Do you know how to use a compass, Dad?"

"A compass? No, but that doesn't matter. A

man named Arthur Maxwell is supposed to meet us at the airport. He'll be our guide through the tundra."

"I know Arthur," the pilot shouted back to us. "He's an old musher from way back. Knows everything about dogs and sleds. He knows this part of Alaska better than anybody, I guess."

"Maybe he's seen the Abominable Snowman," I suggested.

"How do you know there is such a thing?" Nicole taunted. "We haven't seen any sign of him yet."

"Nicole, people have *seen* him with their own eyes," I replied. "And if there's no such thing, what are we doing here?"

"Some people *say* they've seen him," Nicole said. "Or maybe they *think* they've seen one. I won't believe it until I get more facts."

The plane circled the small town. I played with the zipper on my new Arctic jacket. I'd been hungry a few minutes earlier, but now I was too excited to think about food.

There really is an Abominable Snowman down there, I thought. I know there is. I felt a chill, despite a blast of hot air from the plane's heater.

What if we find him? What will happen then?

What will happen if the Abominable Snowman doesn't like to be photographed?

The plane flew very low now, getting ready to

land. We touched down with a bump and taxied along the runway. The plane lurched as the pilot put on the brakes.

Something big loomed at the end of the runway. Something huge, white, and monstrous.

"Dad, look!" I cried. "I see him! The Abominable Snowman!"

6

The plane squealed to a stop right in front of the big monster.

Dad, Nicole, and the pilot all laughed — at *me*.

I hate that. But I couldn't blame them. The big white monster was a polar bear.

A statue of a polar bear.

"The polar bear is the symbol of the town," the pilot explained.

"Oh," I murmured. I knew I was blushing. I turned away.

"Jordan knew that," Dad said. "He was just playing one of his practical jokes."

"Uh — yeah." I went along with it. "I knew it was a statue all along."

"You did not, Jordan," Nicole said. "You were really scared!"

I punched Nicole in the arm. "I was not! It was a joke."

Dad put an arm around each of us. "Isn't it great

the way these two kid each other?" he said to the pilot.

"If you say so," the pilot replied.

We hopped out of the plane. The pilot opened the cargo hold. Nicole and I grabbed our backpacks.

Dad had brought a huge, airtight trunk for film, cameras, food, sleeping bags, and other supplies. The pilot helped him carry it off the airstrip.

The trunk was so big, Dad could fit inside it. It reminded me of a red plastic coffin.

Iknek Airport was like a tiny wooden house, just two rooms. Two pilots in leather jackets sat at a table playing cards.

A tall, brawny man with dark hair, a thick beard, and leathery skin stood up and crossed the room to greet us. His gray parka hung open over a flannel shirt and deerskin pants.

This must be our guide, I realized.

"Mr. Blake?" the man said to Dad. His voice was low and hoarse. "I'm Arthur Maxwell. Need some help there?" He grabbed one end of the trunk from the pilot.

"This is an awfully big trunk you brought," Arthur added. "Do you really need all this stuff?"

Dad reddened. "I've got a lot of cameras, tripods and things. . . . Well, maybe I overpacked."

Arthur frowned at me and Nicole. "I'd say so."

"Call me Garry," Dad said. "These are my kids, Jordan and Nicole." He nodded toward us.

Nicole said "Hi," and I added, "Nice to meet you." I can be polite when I have to be.

Arthur stared at us. Then he grunted.

"You didn't mention kids," he mumbled to Dad after a minute.

"I'm sure I did," Dad protested.

"I don't remember it," Arthur replied, frowning.

Everyone was silent. We pushed through the airport door and started down the muddy road.

"I'm hungry," I said. "Let's go into town and get some food."

"How far is it to town, Arthur?" Dad asked.

"How far?" Arthur echoed. "You're looking at it."

I stared around in surprise. There was only one road. It began at the airport and ended in a pile of snow about two blocks away. A few wooden buildings were sprinkled along it.

"This is it?" I cried.

"It's not Pasadena," Arthur grumbled. "But we call it home."

He led us down the muddy road to a diner called Betty's.

"I guess you're hungry," he grumbled. "Might as well eat a hot meal before we set out."

We settled into a booth by a window. Nicole and I ordered hamburgers, french fries, and Cokes. Dad and Arthur ordered coffee and beef stew.

"I've got a sled and four dogs ready to go," Arthur announced. "The dogs can pull this trunk of yours and the other supplies. We'll walk beside the sled."

"That sounds fine," Dad said.

"Whoa!!" I protested. "We're walking? How far?"

"Ten miles or so," Arthur replied.

"Ten miles!" I'd never walked that far before. "Why do we have to walk? Why can't we take a helicopter or something?"

"Because I want to take photos along the way, Jordan," Dad explained. "The landscape is fascinating. You never know what we'll come across."

Maybe we'll come across the Abominable Snowman, I thought. That would be cool.

Our food arrived. We all ate in silence. Arthur wouldn't look me in the eye. He wouldn't look any of us in the eye. He stared out the window while he ate. Outside on the street, a Jeep drove by.

"Have you ever seen this snow creature we're looking for?" Dad asked Arthur.

Arthur speared a piece of meat with his fork and popped it into his mouth. He chewed. He chewed some more. Dad, Nicole, and I all watched him, waiting for his answer.

Finally he swallowed. "Never seen it," he said. "Heard about it, though. Lots of stories."

I waited to hear one of the stories. But Arthur kept on eating.

I couldn't stand waiting any longer. "What kind of stories?"

He swabbed at some gravy with his bread. He stuffed it into his mouth. Chewed. Swallowed.

"A couple of people in town," he said. "They've seen the monster."

"Where?" Dad asked.

"Out by the big snow ridge," Arthur said. "Beyond the musher's cabin. Where we're staying."

"What does he look like?" I asked.

"They say he's big," Arthur said. "Big and covered with brown fur. You might think he's a bear. But he's not. He walks on two feet like a man."

I shuddered. The Abominable Snowman sounded a lot like a vicious cave monster I saw in a horror movie once.

Arthur shook his head. "Personally, I hope we never find him."

Dad's jaw dropped. "But that's what we're here for. It's my job to find him — if he exists."

"He exists all right," Arthur declared. "Friend of mine — another musher — he was out in a blizzard one day. Ran smack into the snow monster."

"What happened?" I asked.

"You don't want to know." Arthur stuffed more bread into his mouth.

"We certainly do want to know," Dad persisted.

Arthur stroked his beard. "The monster picked up one of the dogs and made off with him. My friend chased after him, trying to get the dog back. Never found him. But he could hear the dog whining. Pitiful howls. Whatever happened to that dog — it sounded pretty bad."

"He's probably a carnivore," Nicole said. "A meat-eater. Most animals around here are. There's so little vegetation — "

I jabbed Nicole. "I want to hear about the snow-man — not your stupid nature facts."

Arthur flashed Nicole an annoyed glance. I figured he was thinking, What planet is *she* from? That's what I'm usually thinking, anyway.

He cleared his throat and continued. "My friend came back to town. He and another guy went out to try and capture the snow monster. Darn foolish, if you ask me."

"What happened to them?" I asked.

"Don't know," Arthur said. "They never came back."

"Huh?" I gaped at the big guide. I swallowed hard. "Excuse me? Did you say they never came back?"

Arthur nodded solemnly. "They never came back."

7

"Maybe they got lost in the tundra," Dad suggested.

"Doubt it," Arthur said. "Those two knew what they were doing. The monster killed them. That's what happened."

He paused to butter another slice of bread.

"Close your mouth, Jordan," Nicole said. "I don't want to look at your chewed-up french fries."

I guess my mouth had been hanging open. I shut it and swallowed.

Arthur seems like a weird guy, I thought. But he's not lying to us. He definitely believes in the Abominable Snowman.

Nicole asked him, "Has anyone else seen the snow monster?"

"Yep. A couple of TV people from New York. They heard about what happened to my friend and came to town to investigate. They set out into the tundra. Never came back, either. We found one of them, frozen to death in a block of ice. Who knows what became of the other.

"Then Mrs. Carter — she lives at the end of Main Street — she saw the snow monster a few days later," Arthur continued in a low voice. "She was looking through her telescope and spied him out in the tundra. He was chewing on bones, she said. Don't believe me, go ask her yourself."

Dad made a noise. I glanced at him. He was trying to keep from laughing.

I didn't see what was so funny. This snow monster sounded pretty scary to me.

Arthur glared at Dad. "You don't have to believe me if you don't want to, Mr. Blake," he said.

"Call me Garry," Dad repeated.

"I'll call you what I please, Mr. Blake," Arthur said sharply. "What I'm telling you is true. That monster is real — and he's a killer! You're taking a big risk, chasing after him. No one has ever caught him. Anyone who goes out after him . . . doesn't return."

"We'll take our chances," Dad said. "I've heard stories like this before, in other parts of the world. Stories about monsters in the jungle or weird creatures in the ocean. So far the stories have never turned out to be true. I have a feeling the Abominable Snowman will be no different."

Part of me really wanted to see the snow creature. But part of me hoped Dad was right. I don't deserve to die, I thought — just because I want to see snow!

"Well," Dad said, wiping his mouth. "Let's get going. Everybody ready?"

"I'm ready," Nicole piped up.

"Me too," I said. I couldn't wait to get out in the snow.

Arthur said nothing. Dad paid the lunch check.

We waited for change. "Dad," I asked, "what if the Abominable Snowman is real? What if we run into him? What will we do?"

He pulled something small and black out of his coat pocket.

"This is a radio transmitter," he explained. "If we get into any kind of trouble out in the wilderness, I can radio the ranger station in town. They'll send a helicopter to rescue us."

"What kind of trouble, Dad?" Nicole asked.

"I'm sure there won't be any trouble," Dad assured us. "But it's good to be prepared for emergencies. Right, Arthur?"

Arthur smacked his lips and cleared his throat. But he didn't reply. I figured he was angry because Dad didn't believe his stories about the snow monster.

Dad returned the radio transmitter to his coat pocket. He left a tip for the waitress. Then we spilled outside into the cold Alaskan air, ready to head out for the frozen tundra.

Was an Abominable Snowman waiting for us somewhere out there?

We would soon find out.

Smack!

Bulls-eye. I hit Nicole in the middle of her backpack with a snowball.

"Dad!" Nicole cried. "Jordan hit me with a snowball!"

Dad had his camera in front of his face, clicking away, as usual. "Good for you, Nicole," he said absently. Nicole rolled her eyes.

Then she ripped off my ski cap. She stuffed it with snow and smushed it on top of my head.

Snow trickled down my face. The cold burned my skin.

At first I thought snow was cool. I could mush it up in my hand to make snowballs. Fall down in it without getting hurt. Put it on my tongue and let it melt into water.

But I was beginning to feel the cold. My toes and fingers were getting numb. We had already walked two miles out of town. When I looked back, I couldn't see it. I could only see snow and sky.

Only eight more miles to the cabin, I thought, wiggling my fingers inside my mittens. Eight more miles! It was going to take forever. And all around us, nothing but snow — miles and miles of it.

Dad and Arthur trudged beside the dogsled. Arthur had brought along four Alaskan huskies — Binko, Rocky, Tin-tin, and Nicole's favorite, Lars. They pulled Dad's big trunk and the other supplies in a long, narrow sled.

Nicole and I each carried a backpack filled with emergency food and other supplies. Just in case, Dad said.

In case of what? I wondered. In case we get lost? In case the dogs run away with the sled? In case the Abominable Snowman captures us?

Dad snapped pictures of the dogs, of us, of Arthur, of the snow.

Nicole threw herself backwards into a snowdrift. "Look — an angel!" she cried, waving her arms up and down.

She jumped up and we checked out the snow angel. "Cool," I admitted. I lay on my back to make one, too. When Nicole came closer to inspect it, I whopped her with a snowball.

"Hey!" she cried. "I'm going to get you for that!"

I leaped up and darted away. The deep snow crunched under my shoes.

Nicole ran after me. We raced ahead of the dogsled.

"Be careful, kids!" Dad called after us. "Stay out of trouble!"

I stumbled in the snow. Nicole pounced on me. I wriggled free and bolted away.

What kind of trouble could we get into? I thought as my feet crunched along. There's nothing but snow for miles around. We couldn't even get *lost* out here!

I turned around and ran backwards, waving at Nicole. "Try and catch me, Miss Factoid!" I teased.

"Name-calling is so immature!" she yelled, chasing after me.

Then she stopped and pointed behind me. "Jordan! Look out!"

"Hey — I'm not falling for that old trick," I called back. I skipped backwards through the snow. I didn't want to take my eyes off her, in case she planned to pelt me with snowballs.

"Jordan, I mean it!" she screamed. "Stop!"

9

Thud!

I landed hard on my back in a pile of snow. "Unh!" I grunted, stunned.

I struggled to catch my breath. Then I stared around me.

I had fallen down some kind of deep crevasse. I sat shivering in the pile of snow, surrounded by narrow cliffs of bluish ice and rock.

I stood and looked up. The opening of the crevasse was at least twenty feet above me. Frantically, I clutched at the icy walls. I grabbed onto a jutting rock and fumbled for a foothold, hoping to climb out.

I hoisted myself up a couple of feet. Then my hand slipped and I slid back to the bottom. I tried again. The ice was too slick.

How would I ever get out of here?

Where were Dad and Nicole? I tried to warm my cheeks with my mittens. Why don't they come to get me? I'm going to freeze down here!

Nicole's face appeared at the top of the crevasse. I'd never been so happy to see her in my life.

"Jordan? Are you all right?"

"Get me out of here!" I shouted.

"Don't worry," Nicole assured me. "Dad's coming."

I leaned against the pit wall. The sunlight didn't reach the bottom. My toes felt ready to break off. They were so cold! I jumped up and down to keep warm.

A few minutes later, I heard Dad's voice. "Jordan? Are you hurt?"

"No, Dad!" I called up to him. He, Nicole, and Arthur all stared down at me from above.

"Arthur is going to lower a rope down to you," Dad instructed. "Hold on to it, and we'll hoist you out of there."

I stepped aside as Arthur tossed one end of a knotted rope into the crevasse. I clutched the rope with my mittened hands.

Arthur shouted, "Heave!"

Dad and Arthur tugged on the rope. I planted my feet in footholds in the ice, bracing myself against the side of the crevasse. The rope slipped out of my hands. I clutched it tighter.

"Hold on, Jordan!" Dad called.

They pulled again. My arms felt as if they were going to be yanked out of their sockets. "Ow!" I cried. "Careful!"

Slowly they hoisted me to the top of the crevasse. I wasn't much help — my feet kept slipping on the icy walls. Dad and Arthur each took one of my hands and dragged me out of the pit.

I lay on the snow, trying to catch my breath.

Dad tested my arms and legs for sprains and breaks. "You sure you're all right?" he asked.

I nodded.

"It was a mistake to haul kids along," Arthur grumbled. "The snow is not as solid as it looks, you know. If we hadn't seen you fall, we never would have found you."

"We've got to be more careful," Dad agreed. "I want you both to stick close to the sled." He leaned over the side of the crevasse and snapped a picture.

I stood up and brushed the snow from the seat of my pants. "I'll be careful from now on," I promised.

"Good," Dad said.

"We'd better push on," Arthur said.

We started walking again across the snow. I gave Nicole a shove once in a while, and she shoved me back. But we were quieter now. Neither of us wanted to end up frozen to death at the bottom of a snow hole.

Dad snapped away as we walked. "How much farther to the cabin?" he asked Arthur.

"Another couple of miles," Arthur replied. He pointed to a steep mountain of snow in the distance. "See that snow rise, about ten miles off? That's where the monster was last spotted."

The Abominable Snowman had been seen by that snow rise, I thought. Where was he now?

Could he see us coming? Was he hiding somewhere, watching us?

I kept my eyes on the snow rise as we walked. It seemed to grow bigger as we came closer to it. The snow rise was dotted with pine trees and boulders.

After about an hour, a tiny brown speck appeared a mile or so away.

"That's the abandoned musher's cabin where we'll stop for the night," Dad explained. He rubbed his gloves together and added, "It sure will be nice to sit by a roaring fire."

I clapped my mittens together to keep the blood flowing through my hands. "I can't wait," I agreed. "It must be minus two thousand degrees out here!"

"Actually, it's about minus ten," Nicole stated. "At least, that's the average temperature for this area at this time of year."

"Thank you, Weather Girl," I joked. "And now for sports. Arthur?"

Arthur frowned into his beard. I guess he didn't get the joke.

He fell behind us a little to check the back of

the sled. Dad turned around to snap Arthur's picture.

"When we get to the musher's cabin I'll take a few more scenery photos," Dad said, as he changed his film. "Maybe I'll photograph the cabin, too. Then we'll all turn in. We have a big day tomorrow."

By the time we reached the cabin it was almost eight o'clock at night.

"Took us too long to get here," Arthur grumbled. "We left town after lunch. It should've taken us about five hours. The kids having *accidents* and all is slowing us down."

Dad stood a few feet away from him, shooting a portrait of Arthur while he talked.

"Mr. Blake, did you hear me?" Arthur growled. "Stop taking my picture!"

"What?" Dad said, letting his camera drop to his chest. "Oh, yeah — the kids. Bet they're hungry."

I explored the musher's cabin. It didn't take long. The tiny wooden shack was empty except for an old wood-burning stove and a couple of broken-down cots.

"Why is the cabin so empty?" Nicole asked.

"Mushers don't stop here anymore," Arthur explained. "They're afraid of the monster."

I didn't like the sound of that. I glanced at Nicole. She rolled her eyes.

Arthur bedded the dogs in a lean-to outside the cabin. The lean-to was a shed built against the back cabin wall. It was filled with straw for the dogs to sleep on. I spotted a rusty old dogsled propped in a corner.

Then Arthur lit a fire and began to fix some supper.

"Tomorrow we'll search for this so-called monster," Dad announced. "Everybody get a good night's sleep."

After supper we crawled into our sleeping bags. I lay awake for a long time, listening to the howling wind outside. Listening for the thudding footsteps of an Abominable Snowman.

"Nicole, get off me!" She rolled over in her sleeping bag and jabbed her elbow into my ribs. I knocked her arm away and snuggled deeper inside my own toasty warm sleeping bag.

Nicole opened her eyes. Bright morning sunshine streamed into the cabin.

"I'll be back in a minute to fix breakfast, kids," Dad said. He sat in a chair, lacing up his snow boots. "First I'm going out to check on the dogs. Arthur went out to feed them a few minutes ago."

He bundled up and stepped outside. I rubbed my nose — it was cold. The fire in the stove had gone out during the night. No one had relit it yet.

I forced myself to climb out of my sleeping bag

and start pulling on clothes. Nicole began dressing, too.

"Do you think there's a hot shower in this dump?" I wondered aloud.

Nicole smirked at me. "You know perfectly well there's no hot shower, Jordan."

"Oh, wow! This is incredible!" I heard Dad's shout from outside.

I jammed my feet into my boots and raced out the door. Nicole pushed right behind me.

Dad stood at the side of the musher's cabin, pointing in shock at the ground.

I gazed down — and saw deep footprints in the snow. Huge footprints. *Enormous* footprints.

So big that only a monster could have made them.

10

"Unbelievable," Dad murmured, staring at the snow.

Arthur hurried over from the lean-to. He stopped when he saw the prints.

"No!" he cried. "He was here!"

His ruddy face grew pale. His jaw trembled with terror.

"We've got to get away from here — now!" he said to Dad in a low, frightened voice.

Dad tried to calm him down. "Hold on a minute. Let's not jump to conclusions."

"We're in terrible danger!" Arthur insisted. "The monster is nearby! He'll rip us all to shreds!"

Nicole knelt in the snow, studying the footprints. "Do you think they're real?" she asked. "Real Abominable Snowman footprints?"

She thinks they're real, I thought. She believes.

Dad knelt beside her. "They look pretty real to me."

Then I saw a light glimmer in his eyes. He lifted his head and squinted at me suspiciously.

I backed away.

"Jordan!" Nicole cried in an accusing voice.

I couldn't help it. I started laughing.

Dad shook his head. "Jordan. I should've known."

"What?" Arthur looked confused — and then angry. "You mean the kid made these prints? It's a joke?"

"I'm afraid so, Arthur," Dad sighed.

Arthur scowled at me. Beneath his beard, his face reddened to the color of a slab of raw steak.

I cowered. I couldn't help it. Arthur scared me. He sure didn't like kids — especially not kids who play jokes.

"I've got work to do," Arthur muttered. He turned and stomped away through the snow.

"Jordan, you crumb," Nicole said. "When did you do it?"

"I woke up early this morning and sneaked out," I admitted. "You were all sleeping. I carved the footprints over my own prints, with my mittens. Then I stepped in the prints on my way back, to cover my tracks.

"You believed," I added, jabbing a finger at Nicole. "For a minute there, you believed in the snow monster."

"I did not!" Nicole protested.

"Yes, you did. I got you to believe!"

I glanced from Nicole's peevish face to Dad's stern one. "Don't you think it's funny?" I asked. "It's just a joke!"

Usually Dad liked my jokes.

Not this time.

"Jordan, we're not at home in Pasadena now. We're out in the middle of nowhere. The wilds of Alaska. Things could get very dangerous. You saw that yesterday when you fell down the crevasse."

I nodded and hung my head.

"I'm serious, Jordan," Dad warned me. "No more practical jokes. I'm here to work. And I don't want anything to happen to you, or Nicole, or any of us. Understood?"

"Yes, Dad."

No one said anything for a minute. Then Dad patted me on the back. "Okay, then. Let's go inside and get some breakfast."

Arthur returned to the cabin a few minutes later. He stamped the snow off his boots, glaring at me.

"You think you're funny," he muttered. "But wait till you see the snowman. Will you be laughing then?"

I swallowed hard.

The answer to his question was no. Definitely no.

11

After breakfast we hitched the dogs to the sled and set off for the snow rise. Arthur wouldn't talk to me and would hardly look at me. I guess he was angry about my joke.

Everybody else has forgiven me, I thought. Why won't he?

Nicole and I walked at the front of the sled with the dogs. Behind me I heard Dad's camera clicking furiously. I knew that meant he'd found something good to photograph. I turned around.

A large herd of elk moved toward us, toward the snow rise. We stopped to watch them.

"Look at them," Dad whispered. "Amazing." He quickly loaded new film into his camera and started snapping away again.

The elk calmly picked their way across the snow, antlers high. They stopped to eat at a stand of bushes. Arthur pulled back the rein on the lead sled dog to keep him from barking.

Suddenly, one elk lifted its head. It seemed to sense something.

The other elk tensed up, too. Then they turned and began to gallop away across the tundra. Their hooves thundered over the snow.

Dad let his camera fall against his chest. "That's strange," he said. "I wonder what happened."

"Something scared them," Arthur said grimly. "It wasn't us. And it wasn't the dogs."

Dad scanned the horizon. "What was it, then?"

We all waited for Arthur's answer. But he only said, "We ought to turn around and head back to town right now."

"We're not going back," Dad insisted. "Not after coming all this way."

Arthur stared at him. "Are you going to take my advice or not?"

"No," Dad replied. "I've got a job to do here. And I've hired you to do a job. We're not going back without a good reason."

"We've *got* a good reason," Arthur insisted. "Only you won't see it that way."

"Push ahead," Dad ordered.

Arthur frowned and shouted "Mush!" to the dogs. The sled began to move. We followed it, on toward the snow rise.

Nicole walked a few feet ahead of me. I picked up a pile of snow and patted it into a ball. But then I thought I'd better not throw it. No one seemed to be in the mood for snowball fights.

We marched through the snow for a couple of hours. I slipped off my mittens and wiggled my fingers. Frost kept collecting on my upper lip. I wiped it away.

We reached a stand of pine trees at the base of the snow rise. Suddenly the dogs stopped short. They began to bark.

"Mush!" Arthur shouted.

The dogs refused to go farther.

Nicole ran up to her favorite dog, Lars. "What is it, Lars? What's the matter?"

Lars howled.

"What's wrong with them?" Dad asked Arthur.

Arthur's face paled again. His hands shook. He stared intently into the trees, squinting into the brightness.

"Something's frightened the dogs," he said. "Look how their fur stands on end."

I patted Lars. It was true. His fur stood straight up. The dog growled.

"Not much scares these dogs," Arthur said. "Whatever it is, it's scaring them bad."

The dogs all howled.

Nicole huddled close to Dad.

"There's something dangerous on that snow rise," Arthur said. "Something dangerous — and very near."

12

"I'm warning you, Mr. Blake," Arthur said. "We've got to go back."

"No way," Dad protested. "We're not going back. I mean it."

The dogs barked and skittered nervously. Arthur shook his head. "I won't go any farther. The dogs won't, either."

Dad shouted, "Mush!" to the dogs. They howled and started backing up.

"Mush!" he cried again. Instead of going forward, the dogs tried to turn around in the snow.

"You're upsetting them," Arthur said. "They won't go any farther — I told you that.

"If we turn around now," Arthur added, "we can make it back to the cabin before it gets too late."

"What are we going to do, Dad?" I asked.

Dad frowned. "Maybe Arthur's right. Something is definitely frightening the dogs. There could be a bear or something nearby."

"Not a bear, Mr. Blake," Arthur insisted. "These dogs are spooked. And so am I."

He marched away across the snow, heading back toward the musher's cabin.

"Arthur!" Dad called. "Come back here!"

Arthur didn't turn around. He didn't say a word. He just kept walking.

He must be really scared, I thought. And that sent a chill of fear down my back.

Still barking excitedly, the dogs pulled the sled around and started following Arthur.

Dad peered into the woods. "I wish I could see what's out there."

"Let's go check it out," I urged. "Whatever it is, it'll probably make a great photo." That usually gets Dad.

He glanced back at Arthur, the dogs, and the sled, rushing toward the cabin. "No — it's too dangerous. We have no choice. Let's go, kids."

We trudged back to the cabin. "Maybe I can persuade Arthur to push on tomorrow," Dad muttered.

I didn't say anything. But I had a feeling it wouldn't be easy to get Arthur to climb that snow rise.

And maybe Arthur was right, I thought. Those dogs really were scared. It was definitely creepy.

Arthur was unhitching the dogs from the sled when we reached the cabin. The dogs had calmed down a lot.

I yanked off my backpack and collapsed on top of my sleeping bag.

"We might as well eat supper," Dad grumbled. I could tell he was in a terrible mood. "Jordan — why don't you and Nicole go gather some firewood. But be careful."

"We will, Dad," Nicole promised.

I stood up and started out of the cabin.

"Jordan!" Dad scolded. "Put your knapsack back on. I don't want you going *anywhere* without it. Understood?"

"We're just going for firewood," I protested. "I'm tired of carrying it. We'll only be gone for a few minutes — and anyway, Nicole is wearing hers."

"No arguments," Dad snapped. "If you get lost, that food could keep you alive until we find you. You leave this cabin, you wear that backpack. Is that clear?"

Boy, was he in a bad mood. "It's clear," I said, strapping on my pack.

Nicole and I crunched across the snow to the nearest trees. They lined a snow ridge about half a mile away.

We climbed the snow ridge. I made it to the top first.

"Nicole — look!"

On the other side of the snow ridge, I saw a frozen stream. The first water we'd seen since we'd set out.

Nicole and I skittered down the ridge and

stared into the icy stream. I tested the ice with my foot.

"Don't step on it, Jordan!" Nicole cried. "You might fall in."

I tapped the ice with the tip of my boot. "It's solid," I told her.

"Still," Nicole said. "Don't take any chances. Dad will kill you if you have another accident."

"I wonder if there are fish swimming under there," I said, staring into the ice.

"We should tell Dad about this," Nicole said. "He might want to photograph it."

We left the stream to gather dead branches under the trees. We lugged them over the snow ridge and back across the snow to the cabin.

"Thanks, kids," Dad said when we burst into the cabin. He took the wood from us and started a fire in the stove. "How about pancakes for supper tonight?"

He's in a better mood now, I thought with relief.

Nicole told Dad about the frozen stream.

"Interesting," Dad said. "I'll go take a look at it after supper. I've got to find *something* to photograph besides all this ice and snow."

The pancakes cheered all of us up — except for Arthur.

He ate a lot, but he didn't say much. He appeared jittery. He dropped his fork on the floor. Muttering to himself, he picked it up and started eating without wiping it off.

When supper was over, Nicole and I helped Dad clean up.

We were gathering up the supplies when the dogs started to bark.

I saw Arthur freeze.

"What's that?" I cried. "What's upset the dogs?"

13

The dogs yelped and barked.

Was someone out there?

An animal? A monster?

"I'll go check," Arthur said solemnly. He pulled on his coat and wool cap and hurried out of the cabin.

Dad grabbed his coat. "Stay here," he instructed Nicole and me. He followed Arthur.

We stared at each other, listening to the yelping dogs. A few seconds later, the barking stopped.

Dad poked his head back into the cabin. "Nothing out there. We don't know what got them upset. But Arthur is calming them down."

Dad grabbed his camera. "You two get some sleep, okay? I'm going to check out that stream. I won't be gone long."

He draped the camera over his fur coat collar. The cabin door slammed behind him.

We heard Dad's footsteps crunching over the

snow. Then silence. Nicole and I climbed into our sleeping bags.

I rolled onto my side, trying to get comfortable. It was after eight o'clock, but still light outside. The sun filtered through the window of the cabin.

The light reminded me of when I was little. Mom used to try to make me take a nap in the afternoon. I never could sleep in the daytime.

I closed my eyes. I opened them. I wasn't sleepy.

I turned my head and glanced at Nicole. She lay on her back, her eyes wide open.

"I can't sleep," I announced.

"Me either," she replied.

I squirmed in my sleeping bag.

"Where's Arthur?" Nicole asked. "I wonder what's taking him so long?"

"I guess he's hanging out with the dogs," I said. "I think he likes them better than he likes us."

"That's for sure," Nicole agreed.

We tossed and turned some more. The sky stayed bright. The light poured in through the cabin window.

"I give up," I groaned. "Let's go outside and build a snowman or something."

"Dad said to stay put."

"We won't go anywhere. We'll stay by the cabin," I assured her.

I crawled out of my sleeping bag and started getting dressed. Nicole sat up.

"We shouldn't," she warned.

"Come on. What could happen?"

She stood up and pulled on her sweater. "If I don't do something, I'll go stir-crazy," she admitted.

We bundled up. I pulled open the cabin door.

"Jordan — wait!" Nicole cried. "You forgot your backpack."

"We're just going out the door," I complained.

"Come on. Dad said we have to. He'll be furious if he finds us outside. And he'll be even more furious if you're not wearing your pack."

"Oh, all right," I grumbled. I hoisted the pack over my shoulders. "Like something's really going to happen to us."

We stepped out into the cold. I kicked at the snow.

Nicole grabbed my coat sleeve. "Listen!" she whispered.

We heard the crunch of footsteps behind the cabin. "It's Arthur," I told her.

We crept around to the back. It *was* Arthur.

He crouched beside the dogsled, hitching up one of the dogs. Two others were already tied to the sled.

"Arthur!" I cried. "What's up?"

Startled, he turned to us. He didn't reply. Instead, he jumped on the back of the sled.

"Mush!" he commanded the dogs at the top of his lungs.

The dogs leaned forward, tugging hard. The sled began to slide away.

"Arthur! Where are you going?" I screamed. "Come back!"

The sled picked up speed.

"Arthur! Arthur!" Nicole and I ran after him, shouting his name.

But the sled raced farther and farther away from us.

Arthur never turned back.

14

Nicole and I chased after the sled, watching it grow tinier and tinier.

"Arthur! Come back!"

"He's got our food!" I cried.

We couldn't let him get away. We ran as fast as we could, our boots falling deep into the snow.

The sled climbed over a tall ridge of snow.

"Stop! Stop!" Nicole screamed. "Please!"

"We can't keep up with the dogs," I gasped.

"We have to try," Nicole cried frantically. "We can't let Arthur leave us here!"

The sled disappeared over the top of the ridge. We clawed our way up. The snow slid under our feet.

By the time we reached the top, Arthur and the dogs were far ahead of us. We watched in horror as they quickly disappeared across the tundra.

Exhausted, I collapsed in the snow. "They're getting away," I choked out.

"Jordan, get up!" Nicole pleaded.

"We can't catch him," I moaned.

Then Nicole said in a small voice, "Where are we?"

I stood up and gazed around. Snow, snow, snow. All around us, nothing but snow. No landmarks. No sign of the cabin.

Clouds had covered the sun. The wind picked up. Snow began to fall.

I had no idea where we were.

"Which way is the cabin?" I asked in a shrill voice. "Which way did we come?"

We scanned the horizon through the falling snow. I didn't see the cabin anywhere.

Nicole tugged on my arm. "The cabin is that way. Let's go!"

"No!" The snow came down harder and faster, stinging my eyes. I shouted into the wind. "The cabin's the other way! That's not the way we came."

"Look!" Nicole yelled, pointing down. "Our tracks! We'll just follow them home."

We started down the ridge, following the ruts we'd made in the snow. The wind howled, growing stronger.

We followed our own footprints for a short while. It was so hard to see in the falling snow. All white and gray. The whole world. White and gray.

Nicole peered at me through the thick curtain of snow. "I can hardly see you!" she shouted.

We crouched low, searching for our footprints. "They're gone!" I cried. The snow had already covered them up.

Nicole clutched my arm. "Jordan, I'm getting scared."

I was getting scared, too. But I didn't tell Nicole.

"We'll find the cabin," I assured her. "Don't worry. I bet Dad's looking for us right now."

I wished I believed it myself. The wind pelted us with hard, icy snow. I squinted into the wind. Nothing but white. White on white. White on gray.

"Don't let go of me!" I shouted to Nicole.

"What?"

"I said, don't let go of me! We could easily lose each other in the storm!"

She tightened her grip on my arm to show she understood.

"I'm so cold," she shouted. "Let's run!"

We tried to run through the snow, stumbling against the wind. "Dad!" we called out. "Dad!"

I had no idea where we were going — but I knew we had to go somewhere.

"Look!" Nicole cried, pointing through the thick snow. "I think I see something!"

I stared as hard as I could, but I didn't see anything.

Nicole pulled me along. "Come on!" she shouted.

We ran blindly. Suddenly, the ground gave way under our feet.

Still holding onto Nicole, I felt myself being sucked down under the snow.

15

Down we fell. Down into the freezing white.

The snow rushed up, swirled around us.

And buried us.

Another crevasse, I thought. Another deep pit in the snow.

Much deeper than the first.

We both cried out as we landed. Tangled up in each other.

"Get off!" Nicole shrieked. "Where are we? Get off!"

Feeling dazed, I struggled to my feet. Then I grabbed both of her hands and tugged her up.

"Oh no," Nicole groaned.

We both stared up to the top. I could barely make out the gray of the sky, high above our heads.

And all around us, high walls of snow. Powdery snow that blew down on us. I peered up to the top of the pit. Chunks of snow broke off the icy walls. They made soft *thud*s as they landed beside us on the snowy pit floor.

"We're trapped down here!" Nicole wailed. "Dad will never find us. Never!"

I grabbed the shoulders of her coat. A chunk of snow fell off the pit wall and landed on top of my boots. "Try to stay calm," I told her. But my voice trembled as I said it.

"Calm? How can I stay calm?" she demanded shrilly.

"Dad will find us," I said. I wasn't sure I believed it. I swallowed hard, trying to fight down my panic.

"Daaaaaad!" Nicole screamed. She cupped her hands around her mouth, raised her head toward the sky, and screamed at the top of her lungs. "Daaaaaaad! *Daaaaaaaaaad!*"

I clapped a mitten over her mouth.

Too late.

I heard a low rumbling.

The rumbling became a roar as the snow walls began to crack and crumble.

Crumble down. Down on us.

Trembling in horror, I knew what was happening.

Nicole had started an avalanche.

68

16

As sheets of snow tumbled down on us, I grabbed Nicole.

I pushed her against the pit wall. Then I flattened myself against the wall, too.

The snow roared down.

I pressed myself tight against the wall — and to my shock, the wall gave way!

"Ooooh!" I let out a startled cry. Nicole and I tumbled through the side of the pit.

We stumbled forward into total darkness.

I heard a crash behind us. My heart pounding, I turned in time to see the pit fill up. Snow piled over the opening in the wall.

Nicole and I were sealed in. Shut in this dark hole.

Our way out was gone. The pit was gone.

We crouched in the dark tunnel-like opening, trembling, gasping in fright.

"Where are we?" Nicole choked out. "What do we do now?"

"I don't know." I grabbed the wall. We seemed to be in a narrow passageway. The walls around us were made of rock instead of snow.

My eyes adjusted to the darkness. I could see a dim light at the end of the passageway.

"Let's see what's down there," I urged Nicole.

We crawled on our hands and knees through the passage toward the light. The passage ended. We stood up.

We found ourselves in a big cave. The top of the cave towered high above our heads. Water trickled slowly down one of the walls. A dim glow came from somewhere near the back.

"The light must be coming from outside," Nicole said. "That means there's a way out of here."

We crept slowly through the cave. The only sound I could hear was the *drip, drip, drip* of melting icicles.

Soon we'll be out of here, I thought. "Jordan," she whispered. "Look!"

On the floor of the cave I could make out a footprint. A gigantic footprint. Bigger than the fake one I'd made in the snow that morning.

Five of my shoes could fit inside that footprint.

I took a few steps — and saw another footprint.

Nicole grabbed my arm.

"Do you think it's . . . ?" She stopped.

I knew what she was thinking.

We traced the giant footprints across the cave

70

floor. They led us straight to a shadowy corner in the back — and stopped.

I glanced up.

Nicole gasped.

We both saw it at the same time.

The creature.

The Abominable Snowman!

He loomed over us.

He stood upright like a human, covered in brown fur. Black eyes stared out of an ugly face, half-human, half-gorilla.

He wasn't that tall — about a head taller than me — but he seemed huge. His body was thick and powerful, with gigantic feet and fur-covered hands — as big as baseball gloves.

"We're t-trapped!" Nicole stammered.

She was right.

The entrance behind us had been blocked by the avalanche. There was no way we could slip past this giant creature.

No way.

The Abominable Snowman glared down at us. Then it started to move.

17

My teeth began to chatter.

I squeezed my eyes shut and trembled, waiting for the monster to grab us.

A second passed. Then another.

Nothing happened.

I opened my eyes. The snowman hadn't moved.

Nicole took a step forward. "He's frozen!" she cried.

I blinked in the dim light. "Huh?" It was true. The snowman stood frozen in a huge block of clear ice.

I touched the ice. The monster stood inside it like a statue.

"If he's frozen in ice," I wondered, "then what made those giant footprints?"

Nicole bent down to study the prints. She shuddered again at their huge size.

"They lead right to the block of ice," she declared. "The snowman must have made them somehow."

"Maybe he walked back here and accidently froze," I suggested. I touched the back wall of the cave, where icy water dripped from above.

"Or maybe he goes into the ice to rest," I added. "Like Dracula going to sleep in his coffin at dawn."

I backed away. It was too frightening, being this close to him. But the monster stayed perfectly still under the thick ice.

Nicole leaned close to the ice. "Look at his hands!" she cried. "Or paws, or whatever."

Like the rest of his body, his hands were covered with brown fur. He had thick fingers, like a man's. Jutting out of them were long, sharp claws.

A chill ran down my spine at the sight of those claws. What did he use them for? Ripping wild animals to pieces? Tearing up people who got in his way?

He had powerful legs, with shorter claws on his toes. I studied his face. Fur covered his whole head, except for a circle of hairless skin around his eyes, nose, and mouth. The skin was a pinkish red. His lips were thick and white and set in a mean-looking grimace.

"He's definitely a mammal," Nicole declared. "The fur is a dead giveaway."

I rolled my eyes. "This is no time for biology lessons, Nicole. Wait until Dad sees this. He'll go crazy! If he can get a picture of this, he'll be famous!"

"Yeah," Nicole sighed. "If we can find Dad. If we ever get out of here."

"There's got to be a way out," I said. I moved to a side wall and pressed it with my hands, searching for a hole, a chink in the rock, anything.

After a few minutes I found a tiny crack. "Nicole!" I cried. "I found something!"

She raced to my side. I pointed out the crack in the cave wall. She frowned with disappointment.

"That's just a crack," she said.

"You don't know everything," I protested. "Maybe there's a secret door here. A hidden passage. Or something."

She sighed. "I guess it's worth a shot."

We pressed on the crack. We stuck our fingers into it. We kicked it. I even tried karate-chopping it.

Nothing.

"I hate to break this to you, Jordan," she said. "But I was right. As always. All you found was a crack in the wall."

"Well, keep looking," I snarled. "We've got to get out of here!"

I kept searching. I ran my hands along the wall, my back to the monster.

Suddenly I heard a noise. A loud *crack!*

"Nicole!" I cried. "Did you find something?"

I whirled around. I realized Nicole hadn't made that sound. She stared at the monster in horror.

"What?" I asked her. "What's wrong?"

I heard another *crack!*

"The ice is cracking!" Nicole screamed. "The monster — he's breaking out!"

18

Crack!

The block of ice splintered apart. Nicole and I pressed ourselves against a wall, watching in horror.

The Abominable Snowman burst from the ice. Chunks of ice smashed on the floor and shattered like glass. The snowman shook himself, growling like a wolf.

"Run!" I screamed.

Nicole and I took off. But there was nowhere to go. We scrambled to the other side of the cave — as far away from the monster as we could get.

"The passageway!" I cried. I ducked down and started to crawl through the passage.

Nicole grabbed me.

"Wait! It's blocked! The avalanche — remember?"

Yes. Of course. The way out of the cave was blocked by tons of snow.

Across the cave, the monster uttered a ferocious roar that shook the walls.

Nicole and I cowered in a corner of the cave. I felt her trembling next to me.

"Maybe he didn't see us," I whispered.

"Then why is he roaring?" Nicole whispered back.

The monster twitched his gorilla nose in the air, sniffing.

Oh, no! I thought. Can he smell us from across the cave?

He turned his huge, furry head one way and then the other.

He's searching for us, I realized. He smells us.

"Unh!" he grunted. He stared into a corner of the cave — our corner of the cave.

"Unh!" he grunted again.

"Oh, no!" Nicole moaned. "He sees us!"

The big creature staggered toward us, grunting with each heavy step.

I pressed myself against the cave wall, wishing the cave would swallow us up.

Anything would be better than having *him* swallow us!

The monster kept coming. His footsteps shook the floor of the cave. *Boom, boom, boom.*

We huddled on the floor. We tried to make ourselves as small as we could.

He stopped inches in front of us and roared again. A deafening roar.

"His teeth!" Nicole cried.

I saw them, too. Two rows of huge, razor-sharp teeth.

The monster growled.

And reached for us. His sharp claws flashed.

He swiped at me. I tried to duck away.

The monster snarled in frustration. He reached out again. . . .

He clamped a powerful paw on Nicole's head.

"Help!" Nicole screamed. "He's crushing me!"

19

"Let go of her!" I shrieked.

But I knew I was helpless.

The Abominable Snowman growled and turned Nicole around roughly.

Then he reached behind her and grabbed her backpack. He ripped it off her shoulder with a sharp, hard tug.

"Hey!" I cried in horror.

With one claw he sliced open the canvas backpack. He reached inside. And pulled something out.

A bag. A bag of trail mix.

Nicole and I stared in amazement as he poured the trail mix into his mouth.

"Weird," I choked out. "He likes trail mix."

The monster crumpled up the bag and shifted through Nicole's pack, searching for more.

"That's all there is," Nicole whispered to me.

With an angry growl, the monster tossed Nicole's pack away.

"Now what?" Nicole whispered.

I reached into my own backpack, and with a trembling hand I yanked out my bag of trail mix. I heaved it at the monster.

The bag hit the floor and slid to the monster's feet. He bent down. Grabbed it. Tore it open. And hungrily gulped down the trail mix.

When he finished, I shoved my pack toward him.

He grunted. Then he dumped out my stuff.

No more trail mix.

Uh-oh.

The monster stretched and roared. Then he reached down. With two gigantic arms, he grabbed Nicole and me.

He lifted us up.

He raised us toward his face.

Toward his mouth.

Preparing to eat us.

20

I struggled, but he was too strong. I pounded my fists on his chest. I kicked as hard as I could. He didn't seem to feel it.

He clutched Nicole and me like a couple of dolls.

"Please don't eat us!" I begged. "Please!"

The monster grunted. He draped us both over the crook of one arm. Then he staggered back across the cave, gripping us tightly.

I kicked him in the side. No reaction. Nothing.

"Let go!" I shrieked. "Let us down!"

"Where's he taking us?" Nicole cried, bouncing as the creature tromped across the cave.

Maybe he wants to roast us, I thought grimly. Maybe he doesn't like his kids raw.

He lugged us to the back of the cave. With one powerful swipe of the paw, he knocked a boulder aside. A narrow passage appeared behind it.

Nicole moaned. "Why didn't we see that before? Maybe we could have escaped!"

"Too late now," I groaned.

The snowman pulled us through the passage. We came out into a smaller cave, flooded with light. I glanced up.

Above us I could see the gray sky.

A way out!

Balancing us in one arm, the monster scaled the wall of the cave. With big, lurching steps, he climbed out of the hole.

Cold air blasted me in the face. But the monster's body pulsed with heat.

The blizzard had stopped. Fresh snow covered the tundra.

The monster stumbled through the snow, grunting as he walked.

His gigantic feet sank deep into the snow. But with each huge step he covered a lot of ground.

Where was he taking us? Where?

Maybe he has another cave, I thought with a shudder. A cave with more monsters in it. His friends. They'll all feast on us!

I tried again to break out of the snowman's grip. I kicked and squirmed as hard as I could.

The monster growled. He dug his claws into my side.

"Ow!" I yelped. But I stopped squirming. If I moved, his claws dug deeper.

Poor Dad, I thought sadly. He'll never know what happened to us.

Unless he finds our bones buried in the snow.

Suddenly, I heard barking. A dog!

The Abominable Snowman stopped. He growled and sniffed the air. Then he gently dropped Nicole and me in the snow.

We landed unsteadily on our feet.

Nicole stared at me in surprise.

We started to run, stumbling through the deep snow. I glanced back.

"Is he chasing us?" Nicole asked.

I couldn't be sure. I couldn't see him now. I only saw white.

"Keep running!" I shouted.

Then I saw something familiar in the distance. A brown speck.

I bumped Nicole. "The cabin!"

We ran even faster. If we could just get to the cabin . . .

From the cabin we heard furious barking — the dog Arthur had left behind.

"Dad! Dad!" we shrieked. We burst through the door. "We found him! We found the Abominable Snowman!"

"Dad?"

The cabin stood empty. Empty and bare.

Dad was gone.

21

My eyes darted around the empty cabin.

"Dad? Dad?"

My heart skipped a beat. My throat went dry. Where did he go?

Was he out searching for Nicole and me? Did he get lost in the snow?

"We — we're all alone," I murmured.

Nicole and I ran to the window. A thin layer of snow frosted the pane. We peered out into the bright sunlight.

No sign of Dad.

"At least the snowman didn't follow us," I said.

"Jordan, why did he drop us?" Nicole asked softly.

"I think the barking dog scared him," I replied.

If that dog hadn't barked, what would the monster have done to us?

As the question pushed into my mind, I heard the dog start to bark again. Nicole and I both gasped.

"The snowman — !" I cried. "He's back! Hide!"

We glanced around, frantically searching for a good hiding place. The cabin was so bare — it wouldn't take the monster long to find us.

"Behind the stove!" Nicole urged.

We dashed to the small, square stove and crouched behind it.

Outside the cabin we heard the slow, heavy footsteps of the monster.

Crunch, crunch, crunch. Footsteps over the snow.

Nicole grabbed my hand. We froze, waiting. Listening.

Crunch, crunch.

Please don't come into the cabin, I prayed. Please don't capture us again.

The footsteps stopped outside the door. I squeezed my eyes shut.

The door burst open. A blast of cold air blew into the room.

"Jordan? Nicole?"

Dad!

We jumped out from behind the stove. There stood Dad, with his camera around his neck.

We both ran to him and hugged him. "Dad! I'm so glad it's you!"

"Hi!" he replied. "What's going on, guys? I expected you to be asleep." He glanced around the cabin. "Hey — where's Arthur?"

"He took off!" I cried breathlessly. "He took

the sled. He took all the food and three of the dogs."

"We chased after him," Nicole added. "But he got away."

Dad's face filled with surprise, then horror. "I'd better radio for help. We won't last long without food."

"Dad — listen." I blocked his way to the radio. "Nicole and I — found the Abominable Snowman!"

He sidestepped around me. "This is no time for jokes, Jordan. If we don't get help, we could starve to death out here!"

"He's not joking, Dad," Nicole insisted, tugging Dad's arm. "We really found the snowman. He lives in a cave under the snow."

Dad stopped and studied Nicole. He always believes her. But this time he wasn't sure.

"It's true!" I cried. "Come on — we'll show you!"

Nicole and I tugged him out the door.

"Jordan, if this is one of your tricks, you are going to be in *major* trouble," he warned. "We're in a serious situation here and — "

"Dad, he's not kidding!" Nicole cried impatiently. "Come on!"

We led him out into the snow to the spot where the snowman had dropped us. We pointed out his huge footprints.

"Why should I believe this?" Dad said. "You

faked the snowman's footprints this morning, Jordan. These just look a little bigger."

"Dad, I swear — I didn't make these prints!"

"We'll show you the cave, Dad," Nicole promised. "Follow the footprints. You'll see. It's unbelievable!"

I knew Dad went along with us only because Nicole insisted. He trusted her. She never played jokes on him.

Leaning into the wind, we traced the giant prints across the snow. Dad couldn't resist snapping pictures of them — just in case.

The footsteps led us back to the cave. They stopped at an opening in the ground.

"The cave is down that hole," I told Dad, pointing.

I think Dad believed us now. "Let's go. Check it out," he said.

"Huh?" I cried. "Back down there? To the monster?"

Dad was already sliding down to the cave opening. He reached up to help Nicole climb down.

I hesitated. "Dad — wait. You don't understand. There's a monster down there!"

"Come on, Jordan," Dad urged. "I want to see this for myself."

I had no choice. Dad was going in there no matter what I said. And I didn't want to wait outside alone. I scrambled down to the opening of the cave.

The three of us felt our way along the narrow passage until we reached the mouth of the big cave.

Keeping close together, Dad and Nicole walked in. But I stopped at the entrance and stared into the cave.

"Jordan! Come on!" Dad whispered.

There's a monster in there, I thought with a shudder. A huge monster with long claws and sharp teeth.

We managed to escape from him once. Why are we going back? What's going to happen to us in there?

I had a bad feeling. A very bad feeling.

22

Dad grabbed me by the hand and pulled me into the cave. I heard the drip of icy water against the back wall. I blinked in the darkness.

Where was he? Where was the Abominable Snowman?

I heard Dad's camera clicking away. I tried to stay close to Dad. I cried out when I spotted the snowman. I expected him to roar and lumber after us.

But he stood stiffly, staring straight ahead. Refrozen again. Inside a huge block of ice.

Nicole stepped closer to the block of ice. "How does he do that?"

"This is *amazing*!" Dad cried, snapping picture after picture. *"Incredible!"*

I stared up at the monster's face. He glared out at us from inside the ice. His black eyes glittered, his mouth set in a toothy snarl.

"This is the most amazing discovery in history!"

Dad exclaimed. "Do you realize how famous we are going to be?"

He stopped shooting for a second and peered up at the brown-furred monster.

"Why stop here?" he murmured. "Why go home with nothing but photos? Why not take the snowman himself back to California? Do you know what a sensation that will create?"

"But — how?" Nicole asked.

"He's alive, you know, Dad," I warned. "I mean, he can crack out of that ice. And when he does, it's really scary. I don't think you could control him."

Dad knocked gently on the ice, testing it. "We won't let him out of the ice," he said. "At least not until we've got him under control."

Dad walked all the way around the block of ice, rubbing his chin. "If we cut the ice a bit, it might fit into the supply trunk," he said. "Then we could carry the snowman back to California in the block of ice, locked in the trunk. It's airtight, so the ice won't melt."

He stepped up close to the ice and snapped a few more shots of the snowman's snarling face. "Let's go get the trunk, kids."

"Dad — wait." I didn't like this idea. "You don't understand. The snowman could *rush* us! He let us go once. But why take another chance?"

"Look at his teeth, Dad," Nicole pleaded. "He's so strong, he picked us both up at once!"

"It's worth the risk," Dad insisted. "Neither of you is hurt, right?"

Nicole and I nodded. "Yes, but — "

"Let's go." Dad had made his mind up. He wasn't going to listen to our warnings.

I'd never seen him so excited. As we hurried from the cave, he called to the snowman, "Don't go away — we'll be right back!"

We rushed over the snow to the cabin. Dad pulled the supply trunk outside. It was about six feet long and three feet wide.

"The snowman will fit," he said. "But with him inside the trunk, it will be very heavy."

"We need the dogsled to pull it," Nicole said.

"But Arthur took the sled," I reminded them. "So I guess the deal is off. We'll just have to go home without an Abominable Snowman. Too bad!"

"Maybe there's another sled around some- where," Dad suggested. "This is an old musher's cabin, after all."

I remembered the old sled I'd seen in the dog shed. Nicole had seen it, too. She led Dad to it.

"Fantastic!" Dad cried. "Now let's go get that snowman before he escapes."

We hitched Lars, our only dog, to the old sled and towed the supply trunk to the cave.

Then we crept silently into the cave, pulling the trunk behind us. "Careful, Dad," I warned. "He might have broken out of the ice by now."

But the Abominable Snowman stood where we'd left him, frozen in his block of ice.

Dad began to cut the ice down to size with a hacksaw.

I paced nervously. "Hurry!" I whispered. "He could burst out any minute!"

"This isn't easy," Dad snapped. "I'm working as fast as I can." He hacked away.

Each second felt like an hour to me. I watched the snowman carefully for any signs of movement.

"Dad, do you have to saw so loudly?" I complained. "The noise could wake him up!"

"Relax, Jordan," Dad said. But his voice was tight and shrill, too.

Then I heard a *crack*.

"Look out!" I cried. "He's breaking out!"

Dad straightened up. "*I* cracked the ice a bit, Jordan."

I studied the monster. He hadn't moved.

"Okay, kids," Dad said. "We're ready." Dad had cut the ice into a six-foot-long rectangle. "Help me slide this into the trunk."

I opened the lid of the trunk. Nicole and I helped Dad tip the ice over and gently drop it into the trunk. It just barely fit.

We slid the trunk along the ground to the opening of the cave. Dad tied a rope around it and climbed out of the hole. "I'll tie the rope to the sled," Dad called from above. "That way Lars can help me hoist it out."

"Hey," I whispered to Nicole, "let's sneak some snowballs into the trunk — just for fun. We can throw them at Kyle and Kara when we get home. Snow from the cave of the Abominable Snowman — they'll never top that!"

"No — please. Don't open the trunk," Nicole begged. "We just barely got the snowman inside."

"We can squeeze a few snowballs in," I insisted. I quickly made a bunch of snowballs, packing them tight. Then I cracked open the trunk and slipped them inside, next to the block of ice.

I checked the monster one last time for signs of life. The ice was solid. We were safe.

"They won't melt in there," I said sealing the lid of the trunk shut. We locked it with the bolt and tightened the rope around it. I felt pretty sure the snowman wouldn't be able to break out of there, even if he did crack through the ice.

"Ready?" Dad shouted from up above. "One, two, three — *heave!*"

Dad and Lars tugged on the rope until the chest lifted off the ground. Nicole and I squatted beneath it to help push it up.

"Again!" Dad yelled. "Heave!"

We pushed as hard as we could. "It's so heavy!" Nicole complained.

"Come on, kids!" Dad called. "Push!"

We gave the trunk a shove. Dad and Lars tugged it over the lip of the cave opening.

Dad collapsed in the snow. "Whew," he muttered, wiping his brow. "Well, the hardest part is over."

He helped Nicole and me scramble out.

We all rested a few minutes. Then we dragged the trunk onto the sled. Dad secured it with the rope. Lars pulled the sled back to the cabin.

Once inside, Dad hugged us both. "What a day! What a great day!"

He turned to me. "See, Jordan? Nothing terrible happened."

"We're lucky," I said.

"I'm so sleepy," Nicole complained, sinking onto her sleeping bag.

I glanced out the window. The sun sat high in the sky, as usual. But I knew it had to be very late.

Dad glanced at his watch. "It's almost midnight. You two should get some sleep." He frowned. "I'd hate to wake up here in the morning with no food, though. I'm going to radio for help. You guys can sleep when we get back to town."

"Can we stay in a hotel?" I asked Dad. "In a bed?"

"If we can find one," he promised. He opened his pack, searching for the radio.

He shuffled stuff around in his pack. Then he pulled things out, one by one. A compass. An extra camera. Cans of film. A pair of socks, balled up.

I didn't like the look on his face. He turned the

pack over and dumped everything on the floor. He sifted through it, again, getting frantic.

"Dad? What's the matter?"

When he turned to me, he had a terrified expression on his face. "The radio," he murmured. "It's gone."

23

"No!" Nicole and I both shrieked.

"I don't believe it!" Dad cried, pounding his fist against his empty pack. "Arthur must have taken the radio so we wouldn't report him."

I stomped around the room, frightened and furious. Our dogs, our sled, our food — Arthur had taken them all.

And now the radio.

Did Arthur leave us here to freeze? To starve?

"Calm down, Jordan," Dad said.

"But, Dad — " Nicole interrupted.

Dad shushed her. "Just a second, Nicole. I've got to think of a way out of this." Dad searched the cabin. "Don't panic. Don't panic. Don't panic," he instructed himself.

"But Dad — " Nicole said, tugging at his sleeve.

"Nicole!" I snapped. "We're in huge trouble. We could die out here!"

"Dad!" she insisted. "Listen to me! You

wrapped up the radio last night so it wouldn't freeze. It's in your sleeping bag!"

Dad's mouth dropped open. "You're right!" he cried. He hurried to his sleeping bag and reached inside. He dug into his sleeping bag — and pulled out the radio, wrapped in a wool scarf.

He switched on the radio and fiddled with the dials. "Iknek, Iknek. Come in, Iknek."

Dad asked the Iknek airport to send us a helicopter. He tried to describe where we were.

Nicole and I smiled sleepily at each other.

"We're going home!" she said happily. "Home to sunny, hot Pasadena."

"I'm going to kiss a palm tree!" I declared. "I never want to see snow again."

I had no idea that our snowy adventure was just beginning!

24

"Ahhhh," I sighed. "Feel that sun? Nice and hot."

"The radio said it's a hundred degrees today," Nicole reported.

"I love it!" I beamed. "Love it!"

I slapped more tanning lotion on my chest.

Our Alaska trip all seemed unreal, now that we were home in Pasadena. The cold, the snow, the wind blowing over the rolling white tundra. The snarling, brown-furred Abominable Snowman. It all seemed like a dream.

But I knew it was no dream.

Dad had hidden the trunk with the Abominable Snowman inside the darkroom in the backyard. Every time I passed it, I remembered the trip . . . remembered the creature lying frozen in there — and shivered.

In our swimsuits, Nicole and I caught some rays in the backyard. Good old sunny Pasadena. Where it never, never snowed.

Thank goodness.

Lauren came over to hear about our trip. I wanted to tell her the *whole* story. But Dad told us to keep quiet about it — at least until the snowman was safely settled somewhere.

"I don't believe you two!" Lauren snorted. "A week ago you wouldn't shut up about snow. Now you're letting the sun burn you to a crisp!"

"Well, we did the cold thing and now we're doing the hot thing," I told her. "Anyway, I've seen enough snow to last me the rest of my life."

"Tell me about the trip," Lauren insisted. "Tell me everything!"

"It's a big secret," Nicole told her. She and I exchanged glances.

"Secret? What kind of secret?" Lauren demanded.

Before we could reply, Dad emerged from the darkroom. He squinted in the sunlight. He wore a down jacket, a ski cap, and gloves. He had turned the air-conditioning way up in the darkroom and covered the trunk with ice packs, to keep the snowman cold.

"I'm going into the city now," he announced, removing his coat. Dad had a meeting with some scientists and wildlife experts in Los Angeles.

He wanted to turn the Abominable Snowman over to the right people. He wanted to be sure the snowman would be treated well.

"Are you kids going to be all right while I'm gone?" he asked.

"Of course," Nicole replied. "We survived the Alaskan tundra. I think we can live through one afternoon in our own backyard."

"My mom is home," Lauren said. "She'll be around if we need anything."

"Good." Dad nodded. "Okay, I'm off. But remember — Jordan and Nicole, are you listening? Don't touch the supply trunk. Stay away from it — understood?"

"Gotcha, Dad," I promised.

"All right. I'll bring a pizza home for dinner."

"Good luck, Dad!" Nicole called. I watched him jump into the car and drive off.

"So what's the big secret?" Lauren asked as soon as Dad was gone. "What's in the supply trunk?"

Nicole and I glanced at each other.

"Come on. Spill," Lauren urged. "I won't leave you alone until you tell me."

I couldn't resist. I *had* to tell someone. "We found him. We found him and we brought him back."

"Found who?"

"The snowman!" Nicole exclaimed. "The Abominable Snowman!"

Lauren rolled her eyes. "For sure. And did you find the Tooth Fairy up there, too?"

"Yes, we did," I joked.

"He's lying in the darkroom right now," Nicole told Lauren.

100

Lauren's face twisted in confusion. "Who — the Tooth Fairy?"

"No. The Abominable Snowman. A real one," I said. "Trapped in a block of ice."

Along with four or five snowballs, I thought to myself.

Snowballs I could throw at Lauren. For a nice little surprise.

"Prove it," Lauren challenged us. "You're making it all up. You think you're really funny."

Nicole and I exchanged glances. I knew what she was thinking. Dad had just told us to stay away from the trunk.

"You two are as bad as the Miller twins," Lauren complained.

That did it. "Come on," I said. "We'll show you."

"We'd better not, Jordan," Nicole argued.

"We won't hurt anything," I promised. "We'll just pull open the lid a tiny bit so Lauren can see him. Then we'll slam it shut. No harm done."

I climbed off my lounge chair and started across the lawn to the darkroom. Nicole and Lauren followed me.

I knew they would.

I opened the darkroom door and switched on the light. A blast of cold air swept over me, making my bare chest tingle.

Nicole hesitated in the doorway. "Jordan, maybe we shouldn't."

"Oh, come on, Nicole," Lauren chided. "There's

no Abominable Snowman. You two are ridiculous!"

"We're not ridiculous!" Nicole protested.

"We might as well show her, Nicole," I said.

Nicole didn't reply. She stepped into the darkroom and shut the door.

In my bathing suit, I was shivering from the cold. It was almost like being back in Alaska.

I knelt beside the huge trunk. I unhooked the latches.

Slowly, carefully, I lifted the heavy lid.

Peered inside.

And let out a chilling, bloodcurdling scream of horror.

25

Nicole and Lauren shrieked and leaped back.

Nicole backed into the wall with a *crash*.

Lauren ducked under the developing table.

I couldn't keep a straight face. I started to laugh. "Gotcha!" I cried gleefully. I was so pleased with myself.

I had scared them to death. They were both stiffer than the Abominable Snowman. He lay frozen and still inside his block of ice.

"Jordan — you creep!" Nicole declared angrily. She punched me in the back.

Lauren punched me too. Then she peered into the open trunk.

And let out another scream. "He's real! You — you weren't kidding!" I could see that she was breathing hard.

"It's okay, Lauren," I assured her. "He can't hurt you. He's frozen."

She stepped closer and stared down at him.

"He's huge!" she cried in amazement. "His — his eyes are open. They're so mean-looking!"

"Close the lid, Jordan," Nicole insisted. "Quick. We've seen enough."

"Now do you believe us?" I asked Lauren.

She nodded. "It's . . . awesome!" She shook her head, stunned at the amazing sight.

Before I shut the lid, I sneaked two snowballs out of the bottom of the trunk. Snickering, I passed one to Nicole.

"What's so funny?" Lauren asked suspiciously.

"Nothing," I said. I sealed the lid shut and latched the trunk. That'll hold him, I thought. We're safe. Dad will never know we sneaked a peek at the monster.

We left the darkroom, closing the door carefully behind us.

"That creature is just so awesome!" Lauren exclaimed. "What is your dad going to do with him?"

"We're not sure yet," Nicole replied. "Dad's trying to figure that out."

She held her hands behind her back, hiding the snowball from Lauren. Suddenly she shouted, "Hey, Lauren! Think fast!"

She threw the snowball at Lauren. It missed. *Splat!* It hit a tree.

"Nice shot, ace!" I cried sarcastically.

But then I gaped at the tree in shock.

The snowball — it didn't crumble to the ground.

It started to *grow*!

Thick white snow spread quickly up the tree trunk — and over the branches. Within seconds, the entire tree was covered with snow!

"Wow!" Lauren gasped. "Nicole — how did you do that?"

Nicole and I stared open-mouthed at the snow-covered tree.

I was so stunned, the snowball fell out of my hand.

I jumped back as it hit the ground — and spread!

"Oh, wow!" I shrieked. I watched snow spread over the lawn like a white blanket.

It spread under our bare feet. Over the driveway. Out to the street.

"Ooooh! It's cold!" Nicole wailed, hopping from foot to foot.

"This is too weird!" I cried. "It's a hundred degrees out — and the snow isn't melting! It's spreading — and growing deeper!"

I turned to see Lauren hopping and dancing, whirling around wildly. "Snow! Snow!" she sang. "It's wonderful! Snow in Pasadena!"

"Jordan — " Nicole said quietly. "This isn't right. We should have left this snow in the cave. It isn't normal snow."

Of course she was right. Any cave where an Abominable Snowman lives has got to be a weird place. But how could we have guessed — ?

"Let's build a snowman!" Lauren cried gleefully.

"No!" Nicole warned. "Don't touch it. Don't do anything, Lauren. Not until we've figured this out."

I don't think Lauren heard my sister. She was too excited. She kicked a spray of snow at an evergreen bush. The bush froze over with snow.

"What are we going to do?" I asked Nicole. "What's going to happen when Dad comes home? He'll kill us!"

Nicole shrugged. "Beats me."

"But — but — you're supposed to be the *brain*!" I sputtered.

"This is so cool!" Lauren squealed. "Snow in Pasadena!" She picked up a chunk of snow and started balling it up between her hands.

"Snowball fight!" she shouted.

"Stop it, Lauren!" I cried. "We're in big trouble here. Don't you understand — ?"

Lauren fired the snowball at Nicole.

Instantly, thick white snow spread all over Nicole's body. Covering her. Covering her until she looked like a snowman!

"Nicole!" I cried, running over the snowy ground to her. "Nicole — are you okay?"

I grabbed her arm. Stiff as an icicle.
She was frozen solid!

"Nicole?" I stared into her snow-covered eyes.

"Can you hear me, Nicole? Can you breathe in there? Nicole? Nicole?"

26

"Oh, no!" Lauren shrieked. "What have I done?"

My sister was a statue. A frozen, snow-covered statue.

"Nicole, I'm so sorry," Lauren cried. "Can you hear me? I'm so sorry!"

"Let's take her inside," I suggested frantically. "If we get her in the warm house, maybe we can warm her up."

Lauren grabbed one of Nicole's arms. I grabbed the other. We carefully dragged her stiff body to the house. Her bare toes, hard as ice, left a long trail in the snow.

"She's so freezing!" Lauren cried. "How can we melt the snow?"

"Let's put her next to the oven," I said. "Maybe if we turn it up full blast, the snow will melt."

We stood her in front of the oven. For good measure, I turned on all the burners on top of the stove.

"That ought to do it," I said. A bead of sweat

trickled down my face. From the heat — or from worry?

Lauren and I watched and waited.

Watched and waited.

I didn't move. I didn't breathe.

The snow didn't melt.

"It's not working," Lauren groaned. "Nothing's happening."

I tapped Nicole's arm. Solid ice.

I tried to stay calm. But I felt as if a hundred butterflies were tap dancing in my stomach. "All right, it's not working. We'll have to try something else. Something else . . ."

Tears rolled down Lauren's cheeks. "Like what?" Lauren demanded in a trembling voice.

"Well . . ." I racked my brain for the hottest place I could think of. "The furnace! We'll hold her in front of the furnace."

We dragged Nicole into the furnace shed behind the garage. The snow seemed to weigh a ton. It took all our strength to drag her.

I turned the furnace on full blast. Lauren stood Nicole in front of the open furnace door.

A blast of hot air sent Lauren and me staggering back. "If this doesn't work, nothing will," Lauren sobbed.

The heat roared out of the furnace. I saw reflections of the red flames on Nicole's icy face.

My heart pounding, I watched to see the ice start to drip and the snow slide off her.

But the ice didn't melt. My sister remained a human snow cone.

"Jordan — what are we going to do?" Lauren wailed.

I shook my head, thinking hard. "The furnace isn't working. What else is hot?" I was too scared to think clearly.

"Don't worry, Nicole," Lauren told my frozen sister. "We'll get you out of this — somehow."

I suddenly remembered how warm the Abominable Snowman had felt when he carried us across the Alaskan tundra. There we were, ten degrees below zero, surrounded by deep snow, and heat had poured off the creature's body.

"Come on, Lauren," I ordered. "We're taking her to the darkroom."

Struggling and straining, we dragged Nicole back outside and across the backyard to the darkroom.

"Stay here," I told Lauren. "I'll be right back."

I raced into the kitchen. I pulled open all the cupboards and drawers, desperately searching for one thing — trail mix.

Please, please let there be trail mix somewhere in this house! I prayed.

"Yes!" I found a plastic bag of trail mix behind an old box of spaghetti. I grabbed it and flew back to the darkroom.

110

Lauren stared at the bag in my hand. "What's that?"

"Trail mix."

"Trail mix? Jordan, can't you wait to eat later?"

"It's not for me — it's for *him*." I motioned at the trunk.

"What?"

I unlatched the trunk and pulled it open. The Abominable Snowman lay inside as before, frozen in the block of ice.

I grabbed a handful of trail mix and waved it above the snowman's face. "Wake up!" I begged. "Please wake up! Look — I brought you some trail mix!"

"Jordan — have you totally lost it?" Lauren screeched. "What on earth are you doing?"

"I can't think of any other way to save Nicole!" I cried.

My hand trembled as I frantically waved the trail mix over the snowman. "Come on! You know you love trail mix. Wake up! Please wake up! Come out and help us."

I leaned over, staring hard at the monster's eyes. Watching for him to blink. Watching for any signs of life.

But the eyes didn't move. The creature stared lifelessly up through the block of ice.

I refused to give up.

"Yum, yum!" I shouted, my voice high and wild.

"Trail mix! Boy, is that good!" I popped a few raisins into my mouth and chewed. "Mmm-mm! Delicious trail mix. So good! So tasty! Come on — wake up and try some!"

"He's not moving!" Lauren sobbed. "Give up, Jordan. It isn't going to work."

27

I jumped when I heard a soft sound. A faint *crick*.

I stared down at the block of ice.

Did the monster move?

No. Silence now. The Abominable Snowman's black eyes glittered up at me, lifeless and blank.

Was it my imagination?

Lauren is right, I thought sadly. My plan isn't working.

Nothing is working.

I gently touched my sister's stiff, frozen arm. Maybe when Dad gets home, I hoped. Maybe he'll think of some way to save her.

"What are we going to *dooooo*?" Lauren sobbed. She was no help at all.

Crack.

I heard it again — louder this time.

And then: *Crrraaaaacccckkkk!*

A long crack ripped across the ice.

The Abominable Snowman groaned.

Lauren leaped back with a wild scream. "It's alive!"

The ice broke up. The furry snowman slowly pulled himself up, moaning.

Lauren cried out in fear. She pressed herself against the darkroom wall. "What's he going to do?"

"Shhh!"

The monster shook shards of broken ice from his shoulders. He lifted himself out of the trunk. He uttered a low growl.

"Jordan, look out!" Lauren cried.

The monster lurched toward me. My heart jumped. I wanted to back away — or *run* away. But I couldn't. I had to stay and help Nicole.

"Unh!" the snowman grunted. He swiped a giant paw at me.

Lauren let out another shrill scream.

I leaped back. What would the monster do?

"Unh!" the monster cried again. He took another swipe.

"Let's get out of here!" Lauren shouted. "He's going to hurt you!"

I wanted to run. But Nicole . . .

The monster swiped at me again — and snatched the bag of trail mix out of my hands.

I suddenly realized that was all he wanted. He had been grabbing for the trail mix.

He poured the trail mix into his mouth, gulping

it down, swallowing it noisily. Then he tossed the bag away.

Lauren pressed her back against the corner of the darkroom. "Make him go back into the trunk!" she cried.

"Are you crazy? How can I do that?"

The snowman growled and staggered across the floor.

His heavy footsteps shook the floor. He stopped in front of Nicole.

He reached his powerful arms around her snow-covered body — and squeezed.

"Stop him!" Lauren screamed. "He's crushing her!"

28

I couldn't move. I stared in horror.

The big creature hugged Nicole hard — so hard that he lifted her off the ground.

"Stop!" I finally choked out. "You're hurting her!"

Without thinking of the danger, I dove forward. I grabbed his furry arms with both hands — and struggled to pull him off my sister.

With an angry grunt, he brushed me away.

I stumbled back — and fell into Lauren.

I turned to see the monster squeezing Nicole.

Lauren pointed down at the floor. "Jordan — look!"

Gazing down, I saw a small puddle under Nicole's feet. Water dripped off her and onto the floor. As it hit the floor, it evaporated. Vanished from sight.

Did I see Nicole's toes wiggle?

Yes!

I stepped closer. Caught a glimpse of her face.

A dot of pink appeared on her cheeks.

Yes!

Chunks of snow dropped off her body. They thudded to the floor, melted, and disappeared.

I turned to Lauren. "It's working!" I cried happily. "He's defrosting her!"

A trembling smile crossed Lauren's worried face.

A few seconds later, the snowman let Nicole go. The ice and snow had all melted and disappeared. The snowman gave a satisfied grunt and stepped back.

Nicole moved her arms stiffly. She rubbed her face, as if she were waking up.

"Nicole!" I cried, grabbing her by the shoulders. Warm. Her shoulders were warm. "Are you okay?"

She shook her head, dazed. "What happened?"

Lauren ran up to Nicole and threw her arms around her. "You were frozen!" she said. "Frozen like a snowman! But thank goodness — you're all right!"

I turned to see the snowman watching us.

"Thank you," I called to him.

I don't know if he understood me. He grunted.

"Let's get out of here," Lauren urged. "I'm freezing!"

"Maybe the sun will warm you up," I told her.

We opened the darkroom door and stepped out-side. The sun still beamed down. The air felt swel-tering hot. But the whole yard was covered in snow.

"Oh, yeah," Lauren murmured. "I forgot about that."

"Hey — !" I cried out when I saw the Abomi-nable Snowman leap out of the darkroom. "He's escaping!" I shrieked.

"Dad will *kill* us!" Nicole cried.

All three of us started shouting at the creature.

He ignored our cries and thudded heavily across the snow. His black eyes narrowed on the snow-covered tree. He stepped up to the tree. Threw his arms around it. And hugged it tightly, just like when he had hugged Nicole.

I watched as the snow began to melt. The blan-ket of white slipped down, down, shrinking away — until the tree stood green and golden again under the sunlight.

"Wow!" I uttered, hands pressed against my face.

But the big, furry creature had more surprises in store.

With a loud grunt, he dropped to the snowy ground. As we stared in surprise, he began to roll in the snow.

The snow appeared to stick to his fur. As he rolled, the snow vanished beneath him.

Before long, the big creature was rolling on green grass. The last of the snow had vanished.

He jumped to his feet. His eyes went wide, and he uttered a pained cry.

"What's the matter with him?" Lauren demanded.

The Abominable Snowman gazed around, stunned, at the green grass, the palm trees. Then he raised his eyes to the blazing sun.

He clutched his fur-covered head and let out a scream of terror.

He seemed confused for a moment. Frightened. Then he let out a deep grunt — and took off down the street. His big paws thudded heavily over the pavement.

I ran after him. "Wait! Come back!"

He tore through someone's yard and kept running.

I gave up. No way I could catch him.

Nicole and Lauren caught up to me. "Where's he going?" Nicole demanded.

"How should I know?" I snapped, struggling to catch my breath.

"I think he's looking for someplace cold," Lauren said.

Nicole agreed. "You're probably right. He must be so hot. Pasadena is no place for an Abominable Snowman."

"He'll probably find a cave in the mountains,"

I said. "It's a lot colder up there. I only hope he finds a way to get trail mix."

We trudged back to our yard. Green again. And hot. I knew that Nicole and I had one word in our minds — D-A-D.

He had instructed us not to touch the trunk. We had ignored his warning.

Now the snowman was gone. Dad's big discovery. Dad's big chance for fame.

Gone. Gone forever.

It was all our fault.

"At least Dad has his photos," I said softly. "The photos will amaze everyone all by themselves."

"I guess so," Nicole replied, biting her bottom lip tensely.

We walked back to the darkroom to close up the supply trunk. I glanced inside the trunk. Two magic snowballs were left.

"Those things are dangerous. We'd better get rid of them," Nicole warned.

"*I'm* not touching them." Lauren backed away.

"You're right," I told my sister. "We should hide them somewhere. They're too dangerous to keep around."

Nicole ran into the house and returned with a heavy-duty garbage bag. "Quick — stuff them in here."

I carefully scooped up each snowball and

dropped it in the trash bag. Then I twisted the bag closed and knotted it tightly.

"Now what?" Lauren asked.

"We should blast them into outer space," Nicole said. "If anyone gets hold of them and starts spreading snow around, we'll be in big trouble. We need the Abominable Snowman to get rid of the snow — and he's gone."

"Pasadena could turn into a ski resort!" I joked. "We could ice skate on Kyle and Kara's swimming pool."

I shivered. I didn't want to think about Kyle and Kara. And I didn't want to think about snow. "We should bury the snowballs," I told them. "But where?"

"Not in *my* yard!" Lauren protested.

I didn't want to bury them in our yard, either. What would happen to them down there? Would they spread snow underground? Would snow spring up through the grass?

We left the darkroom and scanned the area for good burial spots.

"What about the empty lot?" Nicole suggested.

Across the street, right next to Kyle and Kara Miller's house, stood a vacant lot. There was nothing in it but piles of sand and a few empty bottles.

"Perfect," I declared. "No one will ever find the snowballs there."

Nicole hurried to the garage and grabbed a

shovel. We crossed the street, glancing around to make sure no one saw us.

"The coast is clear," I said.

I grabbed the shovel and dug a deep hole in the sand. It took longer than I thought. Sand kept falling back into the hole.

Finally, the hole was deep enough.

Nicole dropped the trash bag into the hole. "Good-bye, snowballs," she said. "Good-bye, Alaska."

I covered the hole with sand. Lauren smoothed it out so you couldn't tell the sand had been dug up.

"Whew," I groaned, wiping the sweat from my face. "I'm glad that's over. Let's go inside and cool off."

I put away the shovel. Then Nicole, Lauren, and I got ourselves some cold apple juice and collapsed in front of the TV.

A short while later, we heard Dad's car pull into the driveway.

"Uh-oh," Lauren gasped. "I think I'd better go home now. See you guys later." She hurried out the back door. "Good luck!" she called. The door slammed behind her.

I gave Nicole a nervous glance. "How angry will Dad be? He finds an amazing, rare creature, brings it home — we let it loose, and it runs away. That's not so bad — *is* it?"

Nicole shuddered. "Maybe if we tell him the *whole* story, he'll be so glad we're not hurt that he won't be angry."

"Uh-huh. Yeah. Maybe."

The front door swung open. "Hey, kids!" Dad called. "I'm home! How's our snowman doing?"

29

We ate supper early that evening. Things were pretty quiet around the dinner table.

"I'm glad you kids are safe and sound," Dad said for the fifth time. "That's what counts."

"Yeah," Nicole said, chewing her pizza.

"Uh-huh," I added quietly. I usually had three slices. Tonight I could barely manage one. And I left the crust on the plate.

Poor Dad. He was trying so hard not to get upset about losing the Abominable Snowman. But Nicole and I knew how bad he felt.

Dad dropped his half-eaten slice of pizza on his plate. "I'll tell the Museum of Natural History that they'll have to make do with the photographs."

"Photographs are better than nothing," I said.

"Better than nothing? Are you crazy?" Nicole cried. "Those pictures are going to amaze the whole world!"

Dad perked up. "That's true. I mentioned them to some TV producers. They went wild."

He stood and carried his plate to the sink. "I think I'll go out to the darkroom and develop that film right now. These pictures are going to cheer me up. I mean, they're historic. Historic!"

I was glad to see Dad snap out of his disappointment. Nicole and I followed him, eager to see the photos.

We sat quietly under the red light while Dad developed the negatives. At last he pulled the first set of contact sheets out of the chemical baths.

Nicole and I leaned close to see the pictures.

"Huh?" Dad uttered an astonished cry.

Snow. Nothing but snow. Ten pictures of snow.

"That's strange," Dad choked out. "I don't remember taking those shots."

Nicole flashed me an evil stare. I knew what she was thinking.

I held my hands up innocently. "I'm not playing any tricks. I swear!"

"You'd better not be, Jordan," Dad warned sternly. "I'm in no mood for kidding around."

Dad turned back to the chemical trays and developed another set of photos. As he pulled them up, dripping wet, we all squinted at them.

More snow. Nothing but snow.

"This can't be happening!" Dad screamed. "The

Abominable Snowman — he should be standing right *there!*" He pointed.

His hands shook as he grabbed the rest of the negatives and held them up to the red light. "The tundra shots came out fine," he declared. "The dogs, the sled, the elk herd — all there. All perfect. All of them. But the shots in the monster's cave — "

His voice trailed off. He shook his head sadly. "I don't get it. I just don't get it. How could this be? Not a single shot of the creature. Not one."

I sighed. I felt so bad for Dad. I felt so bad for all three of us.

No Abominable Snowman. No photos of the Abominable Snowman.

It was almost as if he never existed. As if the whole thing never happened.

Nicole and I left Dad in the darkroom to finish his work.

We trudged around the house to the front. Nicole groaned and grabbed my arm. "Oh, no! Look!"

Across the street in the vacant lot, I saw the Miller twins kneeling down, digging in the sand.

"They're digging up the snowballs!" I gasped.

"Those creeps!" Nicole growled. "They must have been spying on us while we buried them."

"We've got to stop them!" I cried.

126

We hurried across the street, running full speed.

I saw Kyle rip open the garbage bag — and pull out one of the snowballs.

He swung back his arm and aimed at Kara.

"No — Kyle! Stop!" I screamed. "Don't throw it! Stop! Don't throw it, Kyle!"

THWOCK.

About the Author

R.L. STINE is the author of over three dozen best-selling thrillers and mysteries for young people. Recent titles for teenagers include *I Saw You That Night!*, *Call Waiting*, *Halloween Night II*, *The Dead Girlfriend*, and *The Baby-sitter IV*, all published by Scholastic. He is also the author of the *Fear Street* series.

Bob lives in New York City with his wife, Jane, and fifteen-year-old son, Matt.

Add *more*

Goosebumps®

to your collection . . .
A chilling preview of
what's next from
R.L. STINE

HOW I GOT MY
SHRUNKEN HEAD

3

That night before going to bed, I placed the head on my dresser. I brushed its thick black hair straight back. The forehead was dark green and wrinkled like a prune. The glassy black eyes stared straight ahead.

Carolyn told me that the head was over one hundred years old. I leaned against the dresser and stared at it. It was so hard to believe that it had once belonged to a real person.

Yuck.

How had the guy lost his head? I wondered.

And who decided to shrink it? And who kept it after it was shrunk?

I wished Aunt Benna were here. She would explain everything to me.

Carolyn was sleeping in the guest room down the hall. We had sat in the living room, talking about Aunt Benna all night. Carolyn described the work Aunt Benna was doing on the jungle island.

And the amazing things she was finding there on Baladora.

My aunt Benna is a pretty famous scientist. She has been on Baladora for nearly ten years. She studies the animals in the jungle. And the plant life, too.

I loved listening to Carolyn's stories. It was as if my *Jungle King* computer game had come to life.

Jessica kept wanting to play with my shrunken head. But I wouldn't let her. She had already put a scratch on its ear.

"It's not a toy. It's a human head," I told my sister.

"I'll trade you two of my Koosh balls for it," Jessica offered.

Was she *crazy*?

Why would I trade a valuable treasure like this for two Koosh balls?

Sometimes I worried about Jessica.

At ten o'clock, Mom sent me up to my room. "Carolyn and I have some things to talk about," she announced. I said good night and made my way upstairs.

I placed the shrunken head on my dresser and changed into my pajamas. The dark eyes in the head appeared to flash for a second when I turned out the lights.

I climbed into bed and pulled up the covers. Silvery moonlight washed into the room from the bedroom window. In the bright moonlight, I could see the head clearly, staring at me from the dresser top, bathed in shadows.

What a horrible sneer on its face, I thought with a shiver. Why is it locked in such a frightening expression?

I answered my own question: You wouldn't smile either, Mark, if someone shrunk your head!

I fell asleep staring at the ugly little head.

I slept heavily, without any dreams.

I don't know how long I slept. But sometime in the middle of the night, I was awakened by a terrifying whisper.

"Mark . . . Mark . . . "

4

"Mark . . . Mark . . . "

The eerie whisper grew louder.

I sat straight up, and my eyes shot open. And in the heavy darkness, I saw Jessica, standing beside the bed.

"Mark . . . Mark . . . " she whispered, tugging my pajama sleeve.

I swallowed hard. My heart pounded. "Huh? You? What's your problem?"

"I-I had a bad dream," she stammered. "And I fell out of bed."

Jessica falls out of bed at least once a week. Mom says she's going to build a tall fence around Jessica's bed to keep her in. Or else buy her a king-size bed.

"I need a drink of water," she whispered, still tugging my sleeve.

I groaned and pulled my arm away. "Well, go downstairs and get it. You're not a baby," I growled.

"I'm scared." She grabbed my hand and pulled. "You have to come with me."

"Jessica — !" I started to protest. But why bother? Whenever Jessica has a scary dream, I end up taking her downstairs for a glass of water.

I climbed out of bed and led the way to the door. We both stopped in front of the dresser. The shrunken head stared out at us in the darkness.

"I think that head gave me bad dreams," Jessica whispered softly.

"Don't blame the head," I replied, yawning. "You have bad dreams just about every night — remember? It's because you have a sick mind."

"Do not!" she cried angrily. She punched my shoulder. Hard.

"If you hit me, I won't get you a drink," I told her.

She reached out a finger and poked the shrunken head on one of its wrinkled cheeks. "Yuck. It feels like leather. It doesn't feel like skin."

"I guess heads get hard when you shrink them," I said, straightening the thick tuft of black hair.

"Why did Aunt Benna send you a shrunken head and not send me one?" Jessica asked.

I shrugged. "Beats me." We tiptoed out into the hall and turned toward the stairs. "Maybe it's because Aunt Benna doesn't remember you. The last time she visited us, you were just a baby. I was only four."

"Aunt Benna remembers me," Jessica replied. She loves to argue.

"Well, maybe she thinks that girls don't like shrunken heads," I said. We made our way down to the kitchen. The stairs squeaked under our bare feet.

"Girls like shrunken heads," Jessica argued. "I know I do. They're cool."

I filled a glass with water and handed it to her. She made gulping sounds as she drank. "You'll share your head with me — right?" she asked.

"No way," I told her.

How do you share a head?

We made our way back upstairs in the darkness. I took her to her room and tucked her in. Then I crept back to my room and slipped into bed.

I yawned and pulled the covers up to my chin.

I shut my eyes, but opened them again quickly. What was that yellow light across the room?

Squinting across the room, I saw that it wasn't a light. The head. The shrunken head — it was glowing!

As if bright flames surrounded it. A shimmering yellow glow.

And in the glow, I saw the dark eyes gleam and sparkle.

And then the lips — the thin, dry lips that had been set in a hard scowl — the lips began to twitch. And the mouth pulled up in a horrifying smile.

GET
Goosebumps®
by R.L. Stine

❏ BAB47745-5 **#23 Return of the Mummy** $3.50

❏ BAB48354-4 **#24 Phantom of the Auditorium** $3.50

❏ BAB48355-2 **#25 Attack of the Mutant** $3.50

❏ BAB48350-1 **#26 My Hairiest Adventure** $3.50

❏ BAB48351-X **#27 A Night in Terror Tower** $3.50

❏ BAB48352-8 **#28 The Cuckoo Clock of Doom** $3.50

❏ BAB48347-1 **#29 Monster Blood III** $3.50

❏ BAB48348-X **#30 It Came from Beneath the Sink** $3.50

❏ BAB48349-8 **#31 The Night of the Living Dummy II** $3.50

❏ BAB48344-7 **#32 The Barking Ghost** $3.50

❏ BAB48345-5 **#33 The Horror at Camp Jellyjam** $3.50

❏ BAB48346-3 **#34 Revenge of the Lawn Gnomes** $3.50

❏ BAB48340-4 **#35 A Shocker on Shock Street** $3.50

❏ BAB56873-6 **#36 The Haunted Mask II** $3.50

❏ BAB56874-4 **#37 The Headless Ghost** $3.50

❏ BAB56875-2 **#38 The Abominable Snowman
of Pasadena** $3.50